MW00782506

Boy

In

The

Air

BOY IN THE AIR

Don Bajema

©1990 2.13.61 Publications

SECOND PRINTING

ISBN # 1–880985–06–3

2.13.61
P.O. BOX 1910 · LOS ANGELES ·
CALIFORNIA · 90078 · USA

2.13.61 INFO HOTLINE #: (213)969-8043

2.13.61
29 Beethoven St.
London W10 4LG
UNITED KINGDOM

Other books from 2.13.61:

ROLLINS
NOW WATCH HIM DIE
SEE A GROWN MAN CRY
BLACK COFFEE BLUES
HIGH ADVENTURE IN THE GREAT OUTDOORS
ART TO CHOKE HEARTS & PISSING IN THE GENE POOL
BANG!
ONE FROM NONE

BILL SHIELDS
THE SOUTHEAST ASIAN BOOK OF THE DEAD
HUMAN SHRAPNEL

EXENE CERVENKA
VIRTUAL UNREALITY
JUST ANOTHER WAR (w/ KEN JARECKE)

NICK CAVE
KING INK

FR-101
CANTA
The Canta
approxima
highway,
park alon
this peace

remember

BOY IN THE AIR

ROCK-A-BILLIES

They were rough, wild-humored Texans. Their house rang with laughter and singing, steamed with heart-felt conflict, occasionally spattered with their blood. That house rocked with a lust for the next expression of love, the next fight, the next joke to sum it all up. Five kids raving under the roof of two Rebels. They left their pit bulls in Waco, moved out to San Diego and put a beagle named Chino in the backyard. But the blood lust and heart of those pit bulls seemed as much a part of them as the black Indian eyes of their mother, and the sloping shoulders and wry squint of their old man.

They had audacious courage, stubborn determination, and a fierce brotherhood, because they kept their dead alive. In fact they were on a first name basis with death. He was like a visiting uncle who carried a straight razor and told glorious stories as he bounced each of us on his knee. He appeared in cars late at night, across the border in brothels, in the bottle, or staring at us with blood-red eyes. His were stories sung to the slow low keys of the piano at night, or told with laughter in the kitchen by day.

When our thirst raged hotter than water could quench, they'd take me to the ancient well that keeps the souls of our past beneath its surface. When I took their dare and peered over the edge down onto that black pool, one of them would slap my back and holler, "See, there it is" – I'd see my own reflection. We each took our turn pulling to the surface another song, pouring out another story. We'd fill ourselves with the desire to accept the next dare by gulping the cold elixir of our unique American heritage; part romantic, part psychopathic.

Until this very day when my heart drops into a dry hollow pit, or during those times it beats with the universe, or even when I'm just catching my breath, I hear a slow rhythm of inhalation and exhalation, a whisper of inspiration from those down in that well. When I fail to live as the man I was born to be, I hear a chorus of low moans as they recall their own regrets, before their time here expired.

We can't see our ghosts, but we can hear them. When their voices echo in our songs, in our blues, in our dreams, it's our own voice we're hearing. Because they were who we are, and what happened to them, happened to us.

Gettysburg. Still Breathing Ghosts.

Promise them the love of God and county; then watch them become the sons of Satan, transformed by the alchemy of war, from boys crying for their mothers into their brothers' butchers. Pit them. Long after you are sick of the sound of the victor and the vanquished, long after your heart is broken observing their astonishing efforts to prolong a life no longer worth living, you'll hear their last song. It'll sound just like a rebel yell.

I'm one of those still-breathing ghosts. The last few battles, I remember pinning my father's name under my gray jacket. I wanted to go home one way or the other. I did the same thing for a few boys new to the regiment who had not seen this kind of fighting before. Without ammunition, we'd have to run more boys at them than they could kill all at once, and get it down to hand-to-hand just as fast as possible. These new boys' hands shook so badly I penned their names in for them. They said their fingers were too cold. I took it as a white lie. We'd get up in the morning and vomit, squat somewhere and empty our bowels and do the things you might imagine a body has to do when it is expecting to die, beside itself with numbing fear.

The older boys start yelling curses across the pasture. The answer returns in the form of a collected jeer filling the black field. The sound of voices preparing for battle drifts disembodied across the low morning fog. The momentum for hysteria builds into a peak as the fingers of the sun clutch another morning. The quiet fear in the darkness comes to light and thousands of men and boys begin to take the first steps toward true wrathful bloody passion. You'll need it, believe me, when men are killing each other by the thousands in a ten-acre pasture on a single summer morning.

I remember I hated the sound of the clubbing and stabbing and crushing. That crunching wrong sound. The evidence of it in my hair, covering my clothes, on my face, under the nails of my hands. I hated the red pile of agony under my feet, clawing at my legs in blind animal panic. You have to teach them that a boot caving in their face is a lot worse than trying to die there quietly. I'm young, fourteen, and not the youngest by far. I've killed boys younger than me. I've pinned their arms to their sides as a couple of men with jack-off voices shouted insanely to "Stickemstickem… stick that little son of bitch…", watching as the boy's white face opened in a shriek for his mother.

I'm one of the last ones left. Since I'm small, they use me to kill the wounded and the dying enemy we leave behind our advancing ranks. It's an important job, because you never want trouble behind you. If a few wounded can somehow mount a move, you can get cut off, surrounded, which is the worst thing that can happen. Some of them were tricky and you had to stay on your toes.

Struggling for each breath of air yourself, you stumble over a field of groaning, wild-eyed men. The man covered in blood, straining on his hands and knees, howling like a hound, shaking his gory beard – kill him. Move over to the boys encouraging each other in some desperate assurance that the fighting is over for them. Kill them. It is too early in the battle for prisoners. Out of the corner of your eye you see a blue uniform crawling fast and resting, then scrabbling again. The man crying for water, and thanking God when he sees your approach, mistaken that you have come to help him – kill him. The man you saw crawling senses your approach and drags his useless legs toward the trees lining the pasture. You hear his gasping breath falling into sequence with your own. Kill him. Stab a dead man just in case. End the sentences of a hundred whispered prayers. Kill, until everyone there is dead, even the ones still breathing.

(San Diego, California. I can almost hear her father singing, "Come a-long and be ma partee doll, Come a-long and be ma partee doll...", as the 45 spun on her record player. Me and the boys waited to play Johnny Horton. The boys wanted to hear "Battle of New Orleans" again, I wanted to hear "All for the Love of a Girl." A few years later, August 4, 1962...)

BAD GIRL FROM TEXAS

It's about noon, and already over 100 degrees. The novelty of this kind of heat has the energy level climbing all over this Southern California town.

The bad girl from Texas must be making a ragged terrycloth robe very happy as it clings tightly around her body. She is fifteen. She hasn't been to bed yet. One hand clasps the robe in a knot under her throat. The other hand holds a garden hose; its mouth is open, and a clear cylinder splash splatters a torrent into the mud which surrounds some geraniums.

Eddie Burnett is tall, thin, and thirteen. Moments ago he woke up startled, kicked off his semen-stained sheets, pulled the oversized white T-shirt over his head, yanked on the Levis that lay on his bedroom floor, and walked barefooted into the street.

Eddie is approaching her from a few houses up the street, watching her profile bent over at the waist, the robe contouring her hips. She knows he knows who she is and she's not in the slightest ashamed of it: his friends' bad sister, who had to be sent out of town because the boys up the canyon fought and screamed like cats all night long under her window.

Eddie likes the length of her black hair, which has grown from a short bob to shoulder length in the months since he's seen her. Her voice becomes audible as he gets a few yards closer in a studied nonchalant stroll. She is singing under her breath in a whispering deep register... "Saddest thing in the whole wide world is to see your baby with another girl..."

The sound of her voice draws a feeling from between his legs, not in his dick, but under his balls, inside. It comes as a jolt that nearly lifts him on his toes. His heart begins pounding as he realizes he cannot stop his stride and must pass within a few feet of her to enter his friends' house.

At times like this, Eddie usually looks to some sort of omen. He believes in magic. The moment he sees a smooth brown stone, about the size of his palm, laying near the gutter, he knows exactly what he will do with it. The girl does not see him picking it up. He looks four houses down the street where the cop, who doesn't like Eddie much, lives. The ex-Marine, Sgt. Johnson, loves his Chevy Bel Air. Although he is nowhere to be seen, he has set out his plastic pail, the Turtle Wax, the chamois. In direct line with the shining pride of Sgt. Johnson, and Eddie, is a wooden telephone pole. Eddie knows that if he can hit that pole with the hot stone in his hand, from this distance, then the gods of jasmine, heat-wave nights and bad girls will smile on him. If he dents Sgt. Johnsons' Chevy, he can expect no mercy.

Eddie calculated all of this the instant he saw the stone, felt its smooth hot curves fit perfectly against the heel of his hand and his forefinger. He focuses on the pole with the intensity of a cat under a mockingbird. His arm is already drawn back. In a flash his whole body whips outward, and the stone is launched in the final instant of the whirl. Eddie watches the stone climbing in a wide arc, promising all the velocity needed to reach the Chevy, or the telephone pole. As his heart stops in sheer terror, he sees Sgt. Johnson happily swinging open his screen door, heading toward the object of his affection. The stone begins to lose altitude, dropping with a line up on the pole that is deliciously close. Eddie is walking as though he had nothing on his mind. The girl has stood up to her full height and he notes she is a little taller than he is.

Sgt. Johnson hears the stone thunk into the wooden pole. He sees that Burnett kid twisted in a moment of ecstasy, pumping his arm like a home town umpire calling a strike to end a no-hitter.

Eddie regains his composure. The girl looks up toward the source of the sound of the impact. She locks eyes with Sgt. Johnson for an instant, noting the confused and suspicious stare on his face. She turns to see Eddie Burnett stepping onto her lawn. He passes without a nod. She shrugs and returns to the search for snails in the geraniums. Sgt. Johnson watches the brown stone bounce along the grass of his sweet-smelling, just-mowed lawn.

Eddie walks to the side of the flat-roofed stucco house, putting a hand on the top slat of the redwood fence as he disappears over it into the bad girls' back yard. She hears the exchange of greetings between Eddie and her little brothers. "Say, Grant, Robert." "Hey, Eddie." "Hot." "Yeah, hotter'n snot." "Play catch?" "Yeah." She walks into the house thinking that Eddie has grown since last summer.

Ten minutes later she's in bed, dreaming about canyons with fire running along their ridges, and boys from the demolition derby driving out of tunnels, cars' back seats in flames, trailing a plume of black smoke.

Late that afternoon she drags herself down the hall. Eddie had it timed by the sun reaching her bedroom window. He told her brothers he was going inside for a glass of water. Grant looked at Robert and shook his head. "Sure," he muttered in contempt. They knew he always drank from a hose outside. There was no reason to go inside unless it was to see their sister.

As he leaned over the sink, with the faucet turned on and pouring water directly into his upturned mouth, he caught a glimpse of her walking to the refrigerator. She was beautiful with a sleep-swollen face, wearing a huge T-shirt. The smell of Noxzema filled the kitchen. She disappeared into the front room carrying a popsicle and a transistor radio, singing along and harmonizing pretty well with Ronnie Spector. The phone rang and she flew into a rocking chair. One leg crossed over her knee, her bare foot nodding in the air with the song's bass line, she sprawled there until her mother started calling her lazy names. Phone under her chin, she was in the process of making the night's selection. She laughed an intimate laugh and sighed with approval. She hung up the phone and stood on her toes, arms reaching for the ceiling, back arched, T-shirt climbing up her thighs.

Eddie backed out the kitchen door into the dark garage, and into the back yard. Five minutes later the patio screen door swung open and she walked into the full glare of the heatwave, black wrap-around sunglasses, hair hiding most of her face. She answered her mother's calls coming from inside the house.

"In a minute." "I will." "I did." "Oh, I forgot."

Eddie wanted to tell her he'd do anything for her. Steal, lie, leave home, take her anywhere. Instead he played catch with her brother. Without showing the least effort, he threw electric blue lines that smacked into her brother's glove the instant they left his fingers. He knew she could hear the ball hissing from where she slouched against the doorjam. Eddie threw harder. Her brother showed his bravery, standing in front of an eighty-mile-an-hour fastball with a casual blank expression on his face, his eyes as big as saucers. Eddie spoke to her as Grant's return throw popped into his own glove. "Hey, Sis."

She let his words hang in the air, timing her response to the moment before he'd think she was ignoring him. "Eddie, don't throw so hard."

To show her who was king of this street, who ruled her brothers and the other boys around those canyons, Eddie jerked his chin over the back yard fence and he and the brothers vanished in silence for those canyons, and the shore breaks, and the ball parks, and the matinees, and the girls Eddie's age. Girls he lured out at night into the canyons and behind the bushes, or into unlocked cars. Girls who removed his hands from their breasts. Girls who pressed their knees together, or crossed their legs as Eddie felt their sweating faces, and heard their strange throaty whispers telling him, "No. No. No, Eddie." Girls he had been pretending were the bad girl from Texas, ever since she had left town.

BOY IN THE AIR

A stack of books cutting into my forearm, the wind blowing in my face, I'm a seventh grader walking home from school. I've made it a couple of blocks and am presently making my way past the high school athletic field, I'm noticing cars and kids converging with loud chatter and a certain kind of anticipation toward the wide-swung chain-link gate. There must be a couple of hundred kids flowing through that gate and taking their seats in the stands. I won't ask anyone what's going on, but it seems to be something pretty good, although I haven't heard about it. I'm standing in the way, getting jostled, and doing a slow spin trying to balance the stack of books and to "get the hell out of the way," as I am being advised. I manage to get to one side of the river of teenagers and I pretend to be doing something other than trying to find out if it costs money to get in, because I don't have any and I don't need the embarrassment. Most of the time I feel invisible, and in fact I never attract much attention unless I'm in the way. So I stand there shirt tail-out in my Converse All-Stars, my orange hair and freckles, getting tired in the hotter-than-usual April sun. I don't recognize any of these kids, except for one or two of the older brothers or sisters of my friends, who pass by me in silence. I know my place.

Sitting on my books waiting for the crush of kids to lighten, I dig some wax out of my ear casually, burp loudly with a certain aplomb, spread my knees wide and pull my socks up so that my white legs don't show beneath my khaki pants. "Fuck you guys," I think. "I'll rule this place in a couple of years." One of those old Fords that have all the edges rounded out and have dusty, vomited-in-smelling upholstery screeches up and runs over the curb. The Ford is full of girls. Not three in front, and four in the back, but more like five in the front and ten in the back. All the windows are down and arms and an ankle stick out. The radio is loud. The girls are singing "Angel Baby," as loudly and sincerely as possible. I stand up, and put my hand in my pocket. Then I sit back down, resume my former position but twist my butt over so that I can get a better view of them. By now they are untangling and swearing at each other as shoes scrape down unlucky shins, and elbows balance awkwardly and painfully in sensitive newly-formed places. More laughs, and the doors bounce open. If I look up a skirt no one notices and I am poker faced.

I've seen girls in packs before and I know that one does not want to be noticed by them under most circumstances. As they always do, they wait until their full number is standing in a close knot beside the door. Purses are found, hair is brushed, mirrors are flashing, and lipstick is borrowed. This takes 25 seconds. As though by genetic imprint, like a flock of birds, they make the final dress-press with hands, tilt their chins just right, and stroll slowly and silently toward the gate.

I see their calves. Their feet are as big or bigger than mine. They have veins showing in their feet, and the calves are shaved smooth and tanned brown. I breathe deep and notice it before I sigh. I close my mouth and the chestful of air stops at my closed mouth and passes silently out of my nose. My eyes are bugging so I turn toward the opposite direction and notice that the gate area is empty and there is no ticket booth. Okey dokey.

I turn and three of the flock are standing next to me. They are saying something to me. They are asking me an urgent question. They are expecting an answer. I am still sitting on my books. I stand up slowly, gathering my thoughts as though I were a rodeo star recovering from an eight second ride on Oscar. I brush off my butt, why I don't know, and I say, "Huh?" I notice that my eyebrows are somewhere around my hairline and that my voice has squeaked. I clear my throat and compose my face. It doesn't work. The girls are looking at me with a great deal of impatience and they know I am a little jerk. One girl has already given up in disgust. Another one is saying "I said, Is Rick Hanks jumping here today?" I don't have any idea. But I know that someone might see me talking to these high school girls with their women's bodies and I have to somehow prolong the occasion. I do not want to be lacking in anything, information about Rick Hanks, whoever that lucky boy must be, wit, or anything. I get too worked up, and the sentence I begin turns into a stammer. My mouth will not cooperate and it keeps stammering. The best-looking girl looks right over my shoulder and this makes me turn around. I hear her voice saying, "There's the bus." All the girls see the bus from Hoover High pulling into an adjacent parking lot. These are Hoover girls looking for a jumper named Rick Hanks.

My moment has passed. I imagine I hear a "never mind" as the girls disappear but I am probably being kind to myself. I see Junior Osuna looking at me out of the corner of my eye. I stoop to pick up my books and try to act like maybe I'm with these girls and I follow a pace and a half behind them toward the gate. I give that up pretty quick and feel foolish. I then acknowledge Junior with a "Did you see that?" leer behind the girls' backs. But Junior is walking across the street picking his nose. I'm still walking forward with my head turned. I am not looking where I am going, in other words, and manage to stumble in the dirt. This kicks up a fair amount of dust and sand which coats the heel and instep of one of the girls walking in front of me. I bump into her as she empties out her shoe. I mumble an apology. She's so happy to be seeing Rick that she smiles and says, "That's Ok." I melt. She leaves and I look for a place to sit in the stands which are full.

Now I am in front of about a hundred kids and even a few adults. I am facing a sea of faces. I feel like a complete goon. I cannot stand to look for a seat for more than four seconds, I would rather sit on roofing nails. I wander off to the side of the stands and lean on a fence with the little brothers and sisters of the athletes on the field. Little kids. I move to the other side of the stands, walking behind the stands this time and stand near some trees that obstruct most of the view. The place smells to high heaven from the piles of neighbor's dog shit. I am alone at least.

Hoover's track team wears maroon sweats. They are an integrated team of negroes and whites. They are walking in the direction of the field in knots of five or six. The home team wears white sweats and is all white. I wonder which boy is Rick Hanks. I search the 30 or so maroon figures looking for someone who could pull a carload of bitchin' girls to see him jump. I can't tell.

A smallish white boy appears in the bus doorway. All his teammates are on the field. One boy with three coaches steps down the stairs. As soon as he is out of the bus, he smiles a huge smile. The girls in the stands are on their feet yelling "Rick" and waving at him. He is walking like this happens all the time. He breaks into a light trot toward the high jump pit. This is enough to get the girls louder for a second. They sit down in silence, and then they start mumbling to each other. I can hear them. Most of the words are along the line of cute, so cute, or sooo cuuute. Well, cute I don't know, but certainly improbable. He's got a baby face, a Kingston Trio haircut, and with the three other guys he now walks with, he looks like a younger brother. Except for something. What, I don't know. I look into the stands and I can tell that all the Hoover kids are feeling pretty good to be going to the same school as Rick Hanks.

The track is bright in the sunshine, the wind is dying down. There are red, blue, and white plastic triangles hanging in long lines all around the infield. The chalk is in even lines all around the huge track. The hurdles are sitting in stacks by the straight-away. The high jump pit and the pole vault pit are mountains of fragrant wood shavings and sawdust. The athletes are jogging, stretching, jumping up and down, passing batons, and every face looks like it means business. Men in red jackets are carrying pistols. Coaches are standing in conference with clipboards, pointing and directing the occasional athlete that approaches. A man sits at a table with two large loudspeakers, one facing the stands and the other facing the infield. The man at the table shuffles a stack of papers. The stands sound like a gigantic beehive. I am beside myself with energy.

The jumpers take turns warming up by jumping over the bar at a fairly low height. It looks about 5' or 5'6. Well, I should say that the home team jumpers are jumping. The Hoover guys are elsewhere. Finally they join the three white-uniformed jumpers. One Hoover guy jumps a couple of times clearing the bar by a lot, maybe a foot. The home team jumpers begin to sit down. Rick Hanks is over by the football goal post, reading a book. A few minutes later, after the other jumpers have begun to settle down, he appears to be advising his teammates on their approach to the bar and to the take-off area. Each boy stands under the bar and swings his leg up toward it. Some boys do this many times, too many times. It is clear they are trying to appear to know what they are doing, but they seem nervous. Rick Hanks gets a tape measure from one of the coaches and with the help of a teammate stretches it from the near side of the crossbar, out several feet into the grass infield. He sticks an icepick on a measured spot and winds up the tape. One of the other guys returns it to the coach. Rick Hanks stands motionless at the spot. He goes over every inch of the ground leading to the take-off spot – for twenty minutes. He tries out his steps, and then gets the tape measure and measures it all over again. He seems to be staring at the bar. He drops his head and with the first step of his first warm-up jump, everything in the stands, on the field, in the universe stops. Rick Hanks takes nine even steps, smooth and relaxed, with absolute purpose and ease. He does not stop at the take-off spot. His run and take-off combine in a single explosive instant. He shoots lightly into the San Diego sunlight, rises up, passes above the bar immediately, continues rising, rolls slowly hovering high in the air for what seems to be four heartbeats, and slowly descends into the sawdust. He brushes himself off as he returns to his book.

I am sure the girls responded in some manner. I know I heard a couple of hoots from the stands, a smattering of applause, and a grown man yelled something. I am sure that anyone who saw Rick jump that day was happy and inspired to see a boy eventually jump 6'10". But for me the world had not begun to turn yet. I was riveted to the boy reading on the lawn, lying on one side, propped on an elbow, his chin in his hand, his twitching foot the only indication of energy. A boy who knew something. A not-so-special boy who knew how to hover in the air, and do something so beautiful and so dramatic that he could let it speak for him.

(Thoughts after driving past Gorman at 2 a.m. in sleet and rain, semi's tires blinding me in their spray and nobody doing less than ninety. That has nothing to do with the pieces.)

"YOU'RE ON..."

The stakes are always so high. From the very beginning I thought it must be a complex combination of guts, glory, luck, and resolve. But I was looking too hard. If it had been a snake, it would have bit me. All the stakes are high, it shouldn't have thrown me off. As usual, I guess, I wanted it simplified.

It turned out to be more difficult than simply, "Keep your eye on the ball." An old Indian used to drink behind our Little League Park. A home–run was a lost ball. I was still ignoring the warning track in those days. After bouncing my head off the chain link fence with a miracle disguised as the third out stuck in my glove, I lay still on the grass for an eternity. I knew a dramatic moment when I felt one. Slowly I raised my glove above my prostrate body. My dugout, of course, became a Vienna choir of cheers. Ecstatic, and bounding toward my team, I heard the Indian's voice pulling me down to earth, growling, "Relax." I told him to speak to me in English. His laughing fit lasted the next two extra innings. We lost.

For the next few days, the Indian was determined to teach me to hit. He made his own assumptions, I guess. He thought I'd be motivated by his words, had a direction to begin with, and really wanted to hit the ball in the first place. I didn't.

My field of glory was out there. Not in some box with a fat man in black breathing down my neck, pointing out which ball I could have hit. I lived in the field, in the unpredictable moments of defense. I didn't want anything served up, I didn't want to think about a trick pitch. My life was never gonna be a count of three or four.

But the huge face with the purple alcoholic lips kept insisting, "Keep your eye on the ball." I knew it was the wrong advice for me. With a nervous system resounding like a perpetually rung tuning fork, I became a strike-out king. I started swinging the Louisville 31 about the time the dust popped out of the catcher's mitt. I wasn't gonna look harder, I wasn't gonna look at all.

The Indian must have known that. He had to. I was born to live above the letters and below the knee. Out of the strike zone. His advice just turned me on my heels and sent me walking, emptying the Red Hots down my throat, thinking in a whisper.. speak to me in English.

I liked that Indian, I think he was telling me about something he had once but didn't own anymore. It took me a long time to understand it. But now, to this very day, every time a fastball hisses at my heart, I can hear his voice echoing. "Take your base."

Clarity

It rains accidentally, or it rains on purpose. It rains, we know that for sure. At weird intervals, for a moment, or for a couple of celestial days, I'd get it all. I could see it all plain, I'd be absolved of all these sins, I'd have the blessing of cognizance and capacity. I'd be living right then and there. But it evaporates. It leaves no trail. When it's gone, you feel left behind, on fire, in the glare, wishing that clarity would drop out of the sky and soak your long hair, and wash your burning face.

Next Fall

Sex does the same thing. Hours where whatever ground your feet are planted on, the rest of your body is wrapped in the confusing immersion of hers and yours. Warm rapids rolling and bouncing into a flat placid space, revolving slowly in a fainting spin toward the lip of the next fall. Old women whisper about it, saying to anyone who'll listen, that it's just like youth, one day it just doesn't come back. It's gone, except in annoying dreams that make the fabric of their clothes irritate them here, here and here. They look away, and their fingers draw light circles on their soft cheeks, they get up and walk into another room.

The magic of a principled universe has us on our knees anyway, there's no need to bend down. We stand in our gain, and walk to our loss. There's nothing to remember and only ourselves to forget.

(I wrote BLACKROAD on June 16, 1986 and read it that night on KUSF in San Francisco. It was a midnight show. The witching hour. The political climate was pretty discouraging. Sworn enemies of mine were in the White House. I had Yuppies in mind when I wrote it.)

BLACKROAD

When there's nothing left of America to sell, try a piece of blacktop. Just go right out there in the heat of the summer and kick off a hunk or two by the side of the road. Take it back to your doorway, your park bench, your abandoned car. It'll give you something productive to do while you wait for the rest of your life in the two-day-long line, once a month, every month for the maybe-it-works-maybe-it-doesn't anti-AIDS vaccine. And if you can't pay for your vaccine again this month, you can use a chunk of asphalt to help you take the change off the other homeless people you used to step over every day.

You see the beauty of it? It's versatile. Bust out a piece of your car's rearview mirror. Get the light just right and it's as good as a microscope. Now just sit down and get a good long look at that gritty piece of oily shit, that smelly piece of America, that black hunk.

What you have there is the hottest-selling item in the world today. You just need a little imagination. You'll want to catalog the things of value in each piece. And it is rich, and just by association, you are too. Look close. You are holding American nostalgia right there in your hand. You've got product and you can sell it.

Go ahead, collar any fool. Show him the tiny pieces of road kill and hit and run. Little scraps of flesh and hair, feathers and blood – every damn thing that walks, crawls, swims, or flies on this rancid continent is stuck to that tar baby. Minerals? Well, you can pick out a bit of rusting natural resource in any piece; it's standard. Just follow the wasted trail of any romantic redneck who aimed a Bud can at the "Dangerous Curve" sign ahead.

Give your prospective buyer a taste of the shit-splash and piss from the abolitionists and Negroes who were out of place, out of time, out of luck and, with unanswered prayers, hanging right here above this very road. There's probably a faint trace of the marshmallow sandwich from the happy picnic under the kicking feet above.

You can stick a piece next to your pigeon's ear and let him hear the tires screeching out of control from 5,000 prom nights. You'll hear the abruptly ending pleas of the cheerleader's last ride. There's Janis, singing about a drifter who decided to squirt and scram instead of riding along with some trucker trying to remember another song. You can tell that pinched-faced woman trying to sell her kids off to rich folks for a good price that she's already rich if she's holding a piece marked with the treads of the weight of Elvis as he spun the Cadillac around for one more peanut-butter-honey and fried-banana sandwich.

Now that you've got the woman's attention, close the deal. Remind her of the poor boys who jostled shoulder-to-shoulder to Fort Fucking This or That, going to boot camp and getting brainwashed and gung-ho, blistering their knees praying for a chance to kill a Commie for Christ. Sink the hook. Mention those forlorn, lonely flag-draped coffins hiding the addresses stapled to those boys' big toes, as they wind slowly down these black roads back to Momma and Poppa. While Brother and Sis watch the television wondering if Cronkite's box score really matters much anymore.

Remind the techy types that pieces of the space shuttle passed along these roads, big rigs pulling part by part, rutting the asphalt, warning lights flashing to premature takeoff, while coked-out scientists perfected the fuel mixture.

If your mark seems patriotic, you got him in the bag. Just

mention all the politicians who have been rolling down these roads for the past 50 years, checking their maps for the next shopping mall, sitting behind tinted windows with their trousers and BVDs around their ankles deciding which lie has that statesman-like ring. All those millions of moronic hopefuls, racing for the parking lot, smacking their sugar-rushing kids, waiting in the heat like sardines to see a little bit of the history your client is holding in his filthy hand right now. Roads are huge in American politics. Turn to the left, turn to the right. Kennedy got his occipital bone slapped on Elm street like a slung piece of cantalope. You can sell it.

Entertainment? Lennon answered a cop in the back seat as he departed the Dakota for parts unknown, while rain-singing tires spun a last verse of "A Day In The Life." You can sell this. You have the foresight to see the value in this black asphalt, from this long, long dark road. A petroleum product. Everything America has to offer. How do I know? I'm glad you asked.

I saw it myself. I saw a clumsy generation of American dinosaurs dying right here in the middle of the road. Wrinkled knees with ten times the weight of an elephant thudded down on pinkish-raw skin. Scraping for one last time on the hot black grit. I'd been waiting a long time for it. I knew it was coming. I watched as the old giants slowly lifted their fevered heads, saw their eyes go wild with helpless rage. Mouths opening in senile, incomprehensible groans. I could make out their pale faces suspended high in the brown skies, eyes like dim search lights, cataract-blind and tearful. They wobbled over, cursing useless threats, but they coughed up our own young blood. Infecting us. Until we became the same dinosaur ourselves, when the echo of the long hairless necks beating obscenely on the asphalt had time enough to turn into our own nostalgia.

Death shuffled to the East, shuffled to the West, and over us again. We countered clockwise in a slow, dark, circle of power, throbbing to the black bass line of resurrection. We ran blindly on the soft shoulder, screeched around the corner of our ever-present dreams; in a flash, the melted school girl became a white shadow negative.

Clutching our worthless icons, we fought over channels, tried to oppress the world, lost our souls along the highway, became just a fearful guilty hitchiker, screamed each other's names, and jumped eagerly into the fire.

Ask anyone who was there.

MY FATHER HOWLED
IN HIS SLEEP (1953)

My father's hands were still shaking, his lips moved in silent sentences, his red eyes blurred with the tears of his stolen youth. His language was obscured in the mirthless sound of his gut laugh, and slurred with another Pabst Blue Ribbon. His eyes squinted behind the smoke of another Lucky Strike, his mouth softening from a hard snarl to a weak broken smile in the moments he thought I wasn't looking. I was looking. I saw a heartbroken boy who walked like a man.

Snatched off his father's farm by the events of history, he marched willingly under the rumbling thunderheads and into the sunset slash of brutality. My father allowed himself to be trained like a dog to kill, and in that process lost more than he could afford to lose. My father emerged from the nightmare fractured, his soul in pieces.

My father returned to us hollow-eyed, death in a shell of skin, obscured by the ill-fitting uniform. My father lived in a junkyard of human wreckage and tried to make the best of it. My father tore his neck raw against the invisible chain of manhood twisted too tightly, cutting off his inspiration. My father was a dog of war.

(This was the place in 1954 where lonely night-shift nurses and terrified war heroes brought orphans as respectable pets. Here little girls rubbed each other's blue bruises in front of the television set. Outside the boys drew blood in an endless rockfight, while Nike missiles searched the sky constantly, buzzing their electrical mantra as they adjusted their blind aim at unseen and unhated enemies above. Fathers taught sons choke holds, and the competition was for who could raise the toughest kid. A trailer park for the shell shock victims of World War II and their dependents, set on a Tuscarora Reservation in Upstate New York.)

JOYCE

A single Airstream trailer sat shining in the envy of the white trash inhabitants of this U.S. military camp. It was the trailer Joyce lived in with her older brother, David, their mother and their troubled father. There was a newly laid asphalt road that led through overgrown forests, ending in a series of shorter roads and four or five rows of pocked, scraped trailers surrounded by marshland and meadow.

On a drizzly morning, in one of those meadows, twenty children were watching some older boys shooting arrows straight up above their heads. David, a broken-toothed 10-year-old, was bent over backward pulling his bow string, aiming for the sky. The bow vibrated under the tension, and the striped, feathered, steel-tipped arrow launched into the mists above us, immediately invisible in the low clouds.

We stood small in the field, our faces upward, eyes squinted against the filtered sun, silent. Suddenly one of us shouted, and we scattered. The arrow spun downward and embedded itself deeply into the soft earth. Wiping our runny noses, and shivering in our soaking pantlegs and shoes, we converged on the arrow like a flock of birds. An older boy pulled the arrow out of the ground, marking the depth it had sunk with his thumb on the shaft. Each older boy took his turn in the contest of whose arrow would drive deeper.

Joyce and I were 5 years old. I had just had my birthday; Joyce had hers at Christmas. I was completely enthralled with the older kids as they once again displayed a power and privilege beyond ours. We were charged with an element of danger. We knew that for a few brief seconds we had no idea where the arrow was falling, or where it would punch into the ground. The older girls took it on themselves to guide the younger kids out of the path of the descending arrow.

As with most of our games, this one began to shift to increasing risk. I watched the older boys rewarded with cheering and backslapping congratulations for standing under the arrow as it descended, delaying their move to safety, as the arrow whispered downward on them. I realized the right to remove the arrow was bestowed on the boy who stood nearest the shaft when it hit the earth. I looked at Joyce, slipped my hand from the hand of the older girl between us, and waited for David to launch the next one.

Another arrow jumped skyward. As it began it's climb, an angry adult voice yanked our collective spirit down from the disappearing arrow to the oppression and threat of our parents. The older children looked to the approaching voice. The bow was flung on the grass, the launcher running toward the edge of the woods as his father gained speed and fury behind him. Other hungover adult voices screamed confusing and conflicting directions.

"Stay where you are, Joyce."

"David, you little son of a bitch, STOP or I'll...."

"Come here. No. NO!! Stay right there."

My eyes strained for the dot to appear above me. Frozen, heart pounding, face skyward, the arrow falling above me. I could hear a faint, growing whistle and whisper. I felt a feathered breath blow on my face, heard a soft thud and the beautiful arrow stood vertical at my feet, its wet feathers shining at my waist.

I stared. It had just been so high, so invisible, moving so fast, and now it was within my grasp. I reached for the smooth, polished shaft. My fingers brushed the red and yellow feathers. I began to pull. I got down on my knees, put both hands on the shaft and slowly it began to slide out of the earth.

I felt a rough hand push me aside. I heard a crack and saw our bow in two pieces, twisting awkwardly on its string in the air. My friend's red-faced father jerked the arrow out of the ground and snapped it over his khaki-trousered knee. I heard a boy saying, "David's gonna get it." Joyce's voice was crying, "Run, David!" and "No, Daddy!" in an even tempo.

The meadow was emptying with stern scoldings, an occasional slap, and tears. My friends' arms were being jerked, little feet were bouncing in the air beside the stamping strides of enraged parents heading back to the trailers. I sat there stunned, with the crying protests of my friends filling the air, feeling the familiar sense of guilt at another thing I couldn't understand.

One of the oldest girls, who made cupcakes of mud for the little girls' pretend tea parties and usually let me wear her old doll's blanket as a cape, took my hand. She was smiling, with her warm hand on the top of my head, saying, "Time to go home."

A few months later, my mother and I were visiting the Airstream. Joyce was inside watching cartoons. David had brand-new sneakers right out of the box. They smelled great and he was singing to himself under his breath, "Paul Parrot, Paul Parrot the shoes you ought to buy, they make your feet run faster, as fast as I can fly." He went outside and sat on the stairs leading to the trailer door. Unsure of myself, I sat on the stair above him. Behind the screen door our mothers sat drinking coffee. Joyce was playing in a chair, watching Bluto make improper advances on Olive Oyl. I watched David and tried to retain as much of his big-boy ways as I could. I watched with envy as he tied his own shoe I saw him clear his throat like the men and spit a rolling little ball into the dust beside the stairs. I asked where he was going.

"Jake's."

I asked, "Could I go?"

He gave the expected answer. "No."

I asked the obvious question. "Why not?"

He gave the only answer. "Because you're too little."

He called into the trailer, "Ma, I'm going to Jake's."

He jumped off the stairs and ran out of the yard, imitating to perfection an internal combustion engine of tremendous horsepower, and buzzed down the dusty lane and around the front of the trailer. I followed watching as little explosions of dirt jumped behind his feet with each stride. It was the first time I was conscious of running. This led to hours of practice running and looking over my shoulder at the tufts of dirt flying behind me.

God and country. Joyce and I took the yellow church bus to Sunday school off base. I enjoyed the clean clothes, Graham crackers, metallic tasting orange juice, and coloring books. Jesus and sheep, more Jesus and sheep. Lights and bushels. Burning bushes. Little Moses floating in his basket. The teacher looked like Peggy Lee, who was at that time singing "Fever" on the Hit Parade. I thought my teacher was Peggy Lee and I began to associate Sunday school with early stirrings of the erotic.

One early August morning, several parents found themselves sitting under canvas awnings, drinking iced coffee and escaping the oven-like trailers. We'd heard the rumor of a plan to caravan cars to the lake in the afternoon and then to a drive-in movie. The word spread from the woods and yard to yard, until the trailers were streaming with picnic baskets being carried to cars. Suntan lotion was smeared over tiny backs and older kids stood in impatient knots as families prepared for the outing. It was the second time in the summer we were heading toward pine needles, cool shade, hot sun, muddy shores, hot dogs – all to be followed with the miraculous treat of a drive-in. In an hour, six carloads were ready.

There was a delay in getting under way. The problem was Joyce. We sat silently, sweating in the cars as, one by one, someone went to the Airstream, opened and closed the door and soon reemerged, smiling, shrugging and shaking their heads. First her mother, then her father, then David, then a neighbor. Then calls from drivers and honking horns. Joyce had locked herself in the bathroom. Just as her father was telling the rest that they'd catch up, my mom disappeared into the trailer. Joyce's embarrassed mother stood by the stairs; her father sat behind the wheel popping a beer with his "church key." A couple of minutes later, my mother came out holding Joyce's hand and smiling. Joyce's chin was quivering and one fist was rubbing an eye.

"She wants to talk to you," Mom said to me. Joyce walked to our Oldsmobile and faced me. I said, "Joyce, let's go." She looked at me and seemed very far away.

I tried again. "Don't ya wanna go?"

With a shamed look on her face and a hint of anger in her voice, she said, "I don't love Jesus."

I was shocked. Of course we loved Jesus. We learned that in Sunday school. And He loved us. But more importantly, Jesus had nothing to do with this trip to the lake. I stared at her. She stared at me. I reached out of the window and she extended her hand.

"C'mon, Joyce."

She looked crushed. It was the first time I saw that look that told me I did not understand something very important.

Mom walked her to her parents' car. Mom stuck her head into the driver's window, her chin resting on her folded arms. Three or four men leaning against the car, drinking beer, listened to what she was saying. Then they exploded in laughter. My mom pulled her head back out and reached one arm inside to pat Joyce on the shoulder. The others took turns hugging and patting Joyce through the window, but her expression never changed. She continued staring at me from a million miles away.

Mom walked over to our car and got into the front seat next to Dad. She was saying, as she slid her bulky hips over the seat, "Joyce had a little problem with Jesus. She doesn't like him watching her go to the bathroom."

Dad laughed a single cough, and switched on the ignition. He turned his shoulder so he faced me, sitting alone in the back seat, as he reversed down the dusty lane saying, "Jesus."

As we passed her, Joyce looked white and more like a painting frozen on a wall than my friend in a car. Her eyes remained on me for a second, and then shifted to the car floor. I thought she looked scared.

On the drive to the lake, the assorted Fairlanes and Plymouths were filled with kids — except ours, since I always threw up in the car. We parked on a huge grass lot facing the lake. My father said disgustedly, "Go wash off."

I weaved my nauseated way to the water's edge, followed closely by Joyce. I walked into the water, submerged, waded to the shore and sat next to her. I stuck my hands in the warm brown mud. She was sitting with her knees drawn up under her chin. We watched her brother lead a pack of bodies blasting full speed into the shallows and stroking out to the raft anchored in the middle of the lake with a riot of older kids lying around, diving and dunking each other. They were followed a few seconds later by a cascade of whooping fathers.

"How come you didn't want to come?" She shrugged. I waited. Nothing. I said, "Jesus sees everything, but He doesn't care." She said, "But I do."

We sat there a minute more in silence. Then she said, "And at night I see Him looking at me through the roof when I'm trying to sleep."

I said, "He looks after us. He loves children." She said, "Why?" I didn't know so I didn't say anything.

We quit talking and began to play. We played hard through the long afternoon and into the early evening. The only interruption was the period just after lunch when we watched the older kids sitting alone, smoking cigarettes at a picnic table, passing the hour which would keep us from drowning from the cramps in the water. The sun got lower in the surrounding hills and our parents were running low on beer, so we packed up a little early and made our way toward the Lakeside Drive-in.

We stopped at a Dairy Queen next to a Piggly Wiggly and got ice cream for us and booze for them. At the drive-in we waited in a long line filled with carloads of teenagers and families. We felt a little superior to some of the younger kids since we were still wearing our bathing suits and they were in their pajamas.

There was a playground under the huge movie screen: monkey bars, swings, teeter-totters, all made of candy striped pipes and set in sand. While we waited for dark, we played with the kids we knew and challenged the ones we didn't. I was getting real excited. It was turning darker and darker. We were with the older kids and no adults were watching us.

Suddenly the lights blinked on and off rapidly. One hundred kids swooped in a sprint toward their cars. Row after row of elevated blinking lights stretched out before us. I was ecstatic. I couldn't feel my body. I was swept up in a wave of kids. To my left Joyce's blond hair was streaming behind her, her legs churning gracefully beside me. I saw kids running ahead of us, being drawn back to our side and then vanishing behind us. We were flying, aware of each other and euphoric in effortless speed. David passed us in a T-shirted, sunburned animal burst, followed by a wake of struggling friends. Joyce and I held our own. Two men were leaning against the side of a car, smoking. As they watched the flock of kids fly by, I heard one say to the other, in a voice with warmth, amusement and admiration, "Jesus, look at those kids run."

My energy doubled and my strides barely hit the ground. My arms cut through the warm summer night. I felt a bursting pride and love of my own life, and for what I would later understand as my generation.

The older kids crammed into one of the Fairlanes. The huge Plymouth settled under the weight of the men. The women spread out in the other Fairlane. Joyce, David and I, shared a Chevy with the three oldest girls. Our Oldsmobile sat empty. We watched the first war movie and fell asleep during the second, film explosions and Asian screams giving way to exhausted dreams. A long time later, we heard voices gently untangling us in the back seats and carrying us to our own cars. Our parents were stumbling out of the cars they shared. We heard loud voices and laughter as Joyce's father backed over one of the speaker stands. Joyce's mother and father yelled at each other for a few seconds, until my mother cursed them and everyone laughed. Our fathers gunned their engines, and we squealed and rocked our way out of the drive-in and onto the black strip of asphalt leading to our colony on the Indian reservation in the woods.

The next morning I woke up and found my father sitting with several adults and two Military Police. My mother was at the stove making coffee and voices were very low. I walked down the hallway and out the screen door. No car was parked in front of the Airstream. It was quiet as a tomb. One of the kids standing in a knot in front of the shining silver home waved me over secretly.

"Did ya hear what happened to Joyce?"

My heart hit a huge beat and froze as she said, "Last night she got killed in her dad's car. He hit a tree. David broke his arm and his leg and he's in the hospital. So's his mom. His dad is in jail."

None of the kids on that base ever went to Sunday school again. And our parents never even mentioned it.

THE WIVES TOOK TURNS

The wife of a shell-shock victim in the trailer park is usually young, and a long way from home. Exhausted, often publicly abused and battered, she tries to keep alive enough spiritually to love some of her several kids as much as possible. Which is not easy. The father's influence over her first son is poisonous. She watches her son agonize, from infancy on, as he is taught to reject the substance of her affection. Affection has no place on a battlefield. If she interferes, she is punished for weakening the boy.

Despite her efforts, including the beatings she must endure when she takes a stand in the boy's interest, she loses contact with him as he struggles to catch up on the trail of his father's violent footsteps. She watches helplessly as her son gradually develops a deep seething rage, which takes the place of the love he feels, but is forced to deny her. A confusing rage that will be submerged, yet extended to his sisters, and eventually to all women. If she has a second son, he will be lost to her even quicker than the first.

She turns to her daughter, who she finds struggling not to repeat her mother's bleak existence. They argue constantly, confused by the need they have for each other, and the self-loathing they feel as their love becomes a mockery in this world ruled by the Army. Eventually the wife accepts her fate, shuffling within the trailer in a semi-stupor of silent compliant slavery. She is heartbroken as she watches the blind desperation of her daughter grow into a perverted attraction for men with the same essential qualities as her own brother and father, beginning her journey toward her own enslavement, and perpetuating the cycle.

In childhood the siblings develop a lifelong communion of fear. They are kept apart by the associations of submerged horror and forgotten cruelty. They are bound by their blood and the memory of their flickering souls, long ago extinguished in the airless childhood of those trailers.

They are afraid to see their mother take another beating. Afraid to take another beating themselves. Afraid of the temporary quiet which in a moment can explode in another unpredictable scene of Father's hysterical, blind, hallucinating, medicated panic. Afraid of the catatonia which fills the low ceiling of the trailer like a storm cloud. They creep around, watching Father as he sits on the edge of his bed in the dark far end of the tunnel, saying nothing, hearing nothing, responding to nothing.

The trailer stinks of terror when Father begins his sixteen-hour confession, filled with the struggling revelations of his broken soul. He tortures his wife with his self-deprecations. Why is she so afraid? Because she knows that in any instant she will see the flip side of her husbands illness. The deprecations will become accusations, the confessions will become denials, the denials will become rationalizations. His rumbling voice will storm in the close confines of the metal tube, and threats and weird plots will hiss into his wife's face. Father will change from a pliant and hopeful invalid into a monster of cold, hard hopeless cruelty. Father will make the dependents suffer. Then the military man will make the wife and children feel a little bit of the fear and pain and rage that is at the heart of his regimented insane world. They'll learn well – because he'll teach them.

The wife will take her turn, in her own desperate need. You'll see her in a scarf, hiding the lumpy cheeks and jaw line. Almost glamorous in her sun-glasses hiding her bloody eyes. She goes to the hospital to arrange an appointment with the base doctor, the highest in command. She tells him she can't take anymore, and asks if they can please take her husband back on the ward. Sometimes they do. But usually the request has to come from her husband or his superior officer, because this is an important decision, a man's decision.

Sometimes the husband discovers the wife's visit and then the wife is hospitalized for a couple of days. The children remain buried under sheets in their bunks, forcing themselves to sleep with high temperatures, unable to set their feet on their father's linoleum floor. They dream of dinosaurs mating in blood and mud under black skies as their drunken father careens against the thin trailer walls muttering, "What did I do – oh baby, – what did I do to you ? I'm sorry – I'm so sorry. You BITCH! You CASTRATING whore."

Normally the doctor just feigns a sympathetic voice and tells the wife the old story. How her husband is in bad shape from the war, and that she just can't understand what he has been through. How much he needs her support, and that he'll be better when he gets back his confidence in himself and the world again. The doctor might even read her husband's war record, and he embellishes it a little. The confused wife wants to believe that her husband is a war hero, that somehow all this slaughter is not in vain. She makes an effort to believe the lie that his sacrifice somehow belittles her own. She starts feeling proud of her man, and guilty about complaining after all he's been through.

Slowly she reaches for her handbag, as she begins to see the image of the young man she married. She walks down the steps of the hospital, adjusts her scarf and sunglasses, and fights bravely the flow of her tears.

She returns home, chilled to the bone in her cold nervous sweat, seeing an old photograph of her husband before her eyes – the farmboy from Lawrence, Kansas with the funny grin, the 4-H president from Tacoma, or the football hero from Amarillo. She'll decide to face another day, and another night. Besides, where could she go with all those kids?

EPITAPH

She walks onto the trailer stair and grabs the cold metal handle. Her breath gasps in her throat as she steps into the dark, into the tomb, into the stench of Jim Beam and beer. She hears a voice like the growl of a dog, somewhere in the darkest corner: "Where the fuck have you been?"

NAVAJO

I had the front seat to myself, windows down, hot air exploding in loud gusts propelling little tornados of paper and dirt around me. The landscape was hot as hell and repeated itself over and over and over.

She was sleeping – taking the backseat on one hip, jet black hair blasting in the wind, swirling around her head all over her face. She was so tired she couldn't feel a thing. With her Navajo eyes closed, she looked Japanese, beautiful as all get out.

The car I was driving was exactly the kind I had always hoped to drive – a real gas-guzzler, with a broken headlight, oversized tires in the rear, and a mass of tangled wires hanging under the dashboard, rumbling along the absolutely abandoned highway. Nothing worked except the gas gauge, and it read empty.

Her dog was thirsty. I twisted over the back seat and felt around with my free hand until I was scratching behind the dog's long, pointed ear. We approached a Texaco station with a faded Pegasus heading forty-five degrees and skyward on a round tin shield.

The car growled as I downshifted. The gravel from the roadside rose in a dusty cloud. I drove past the station, slowed down to around sixty and spun a bootlegger turn back into my own dust cloud, filling the windows with brown grit. The girl rocked against the back seat still sound asleep. The dog tried to get his footing and thumped into the front seat twice. I idled the car into the station's garage and parked it in the empty shade. The dust cloud blew slowly down the road outside. I sat there in the dark, adjusting my eyes and feeling the cool air, thinking of the sun, blinding hot outside of the tin shack, and my wife.

I opened the car door and kissed the air loudly a couple of

times until the dizzy dog pressed unsteady front paws on the greasy concrete. The dog followed me around until I found a bucket and filled it with water. The dog drank in sloppy loud slaps.

I went around the corner of the shack and took a long piss. The car door latch opened and slammed shut. Her voice was cooing to her dog. I began to make out her words. "Where'd he go? Huh? Where'd he go?"

I shook off the last drops and buttoned my pants. She wound around the corner, pulling her waist-length black hair off the side of her face. She rubbed one eye with a small silver-ringed fist, breathed in and out deeply, put her hands in the back of her jeans and settled her weight on one leg, getting her balance in her rough-out boots.

"Where are we?" she demanded with a smile.

I shrugged. "Dunno."

"Good. The less you know the better."

"That's what they tell me." Her teeth gleamed behind dry lips.

We stood awhile looking out across four hundred miles of glaring desert, ending in heat-wave rippling, reddish mountains.

"We're lost, then," she finally muttered. I knew that was a way of referring to how we felt about each other. I knew not to respond. A minute or two passed.

43

"Almost lost. We're heading south. We'll cross a main road before too long. We can be in those hills tonight, or in some beach parking lot by tomorrow morning" My words sounded like a speech and I felt embarrassed. I hoped she wouldn't put me down.

She nodded and said, "Let's go to the beach."

She picked up a stone and dented a fresh beer can lying about forty yards away. I didn't move. She did it again, same beer can. I wiped my nose and covered my smile, in a self-conscious movie-cowboy kind of way.

She leaned under my face and looked up into my eyes, saying in a mocking tone, "I'm magic."

I told her I knew that already, with the same tone I would

use later to ask the ancient man behind the motel office desk if he had a room.

She tossed a stick and the dog chased after it. He brought it back wagging his tail with pride.

She looked at me and said, "Just like you."

"True love," I said, sniffing the air.

(Stage direction. In a spotlight a young girl is tossing a baseball high into the air, and catching it in her worn baseball glove. As the ball ascends it disappears out of the cone of the spotlight, after several beats, it reappears as she catches it. To the girl with the glove the timing seems natural. A woman comes onto the stage and gasps as she sees her. She tries to peer under her hand into the audience, looking confused. The mechanical sound of distant trash trucks crushing garbage fills the room. The trucks start grinding into first gear and the sound continues to come closer. The woman takes center stage. The girl continues throwing and catching. The woman attempts to appear calm, but her nervous hands give her away as she fidgets with her cotton dress.)

BOY IN THE AIR ◆ 10

DOG PARTY

"Well a long time ago, when I was young, the other kids and I were pretty much left up to ourselves – not much supervision or anything. We were all pretending we were happy, watching 'Leave It To Beaver', 'Ozzie and Harriet' but feeling this gnawing loneliness. And this anger. Like it wasn't supposed to be like this, like we were getting tricked. We were always fighting and our fathers always talked about the war. Until we began to feel like targets or something.

"There was a boy living on our street. He had this thing with dogs, ya know? (Pause.) He had an inordinate attraction to them. None of us knew why. We knew he loved them, but still..."

"He was a strange boy with a strange laugh, a fourth-grader with bleeding bite marks and scratches all over his arms. We'd see him following an old lady's cocker spaniel or feeding somebody's mutt through a fence. Calling and crooning – anybody's dog. He'd devote his whole weekend to one dog. We'd need another kid to play outfield, or we'd be alone and want to play catch. Nope. He's got no time. (Girl leaves the stage.) He'd be waiting for Fido. He'd just wait. He was inexhaustible. The dogs knew what was on his mind. They'd hide. The kid knew they knew, and that made it better for him. He'd wait for hours until they made their false move. They'd get hungry and take the bait, or they'd finally give in to the hope against hope that the boy wouldn't really do it. They were wrong. He was quick. He'd grab them and he'd say, 'You fool – I'm going to drown you, Fido.' He called every dog Fido, don't ask me why."

"For a couple of months he did it in secret. But by then we knew he had an odd devotion to dogs. He had witnessed their desperation, he'd watch their losing cause. He weighed each dog's pain threshold. He knew what they could take, he was impressed. He'd stroke them, hold them in his arms as they shook with fear. He'd whisper to them. Then he'd take them to a big 55-gallon drum that his father brought home from the Army base, and drown them. Normally we used the drums for trash cans. I remember he was always so happy on Wednesdays. The trash trucks emptied the cans on Wednesday. (Sound of trash trucks stops.) He called it 'Anything Can Happen Day.' "

"He'd drag the garden hose to the black drums, greasy pieces of who-the-hell-knows-what floating with lettuce and tomato skins. He'd be talking real softly to these desperate, writhing, wimpering dogs. Somehow he'd get one into the spinning water. You don't know how long it takes for a Labrador to drown. You don't measure it in minutes. Eternity is more like it. Eternal moments. They fight like hell. They fight to stay out of hell, swimming that pathetic pointless upright paddle, nose bleeding from the broom handle he used to push them under, pinning them to the bottom. Panic. Wildest eyes you'll ever see. Then, just when they were on the other side, as soon as their bodies stopped struggling and only twitched, he'd rescue them."

"He'd pull them out of the barrel. He'd hold them upside down. Pink water draining out of their mouth and nose. Then it looked like a little light would go on behind their eyes. He'd look relieved and he'd start to cry, saying, "See? There it is!" He'd be smiling at them as they began to figure out where they were. He'd lie down beside them on the ground. They'd be too weak to move. He'd pet them and put his arms around them."

The dogs would think that the boy had saved them, although they would always have a fear of the green garden hose and the barrel. And on Wednesdays after that summer, the whole street would howl when the trash trucks turned the corner. You could see that the dogs sensed something else. Belief, I guess.

"The dogs wanted to believe that the boy had saved them. It was easier than facing what the boy had really done. So they let their memory start from the moment they saw his smiling face. The dogs loved him. Really. They followed him everywhere. If you ever saw him, he'd be with a couple of dogs. All by himself, with a couple of dogs trailing behind him."

"I asked the boy, 'What did you have to do that for?' He looked at me like I was stupid. He said, 'I'm looking for love, something bigger than my life.'"

DASHBOARD

(March 2, 1971 – Santee, California)

"What the fuck should I be trying to write lines for ?" He wiped the running nostril awkwardly with the heel of his hand. His drunken eyes focused on the grimy visor over the filthy dashboard. The 1949 Ford truck bounced over a series of potholes. The drunk's eyelids took a second and a half to raise and lower over his red wet eyes. He turned to the driver. "I can't even play guitar." He thought this remark was very funny. He managed a slack smile to show the driver he got his own joke.

"Can't sing, either. Wish I could, but..." He shook his head with sloppy emphasis, "I can't."

His shoulders twisted to his side window. He stuck his head outside the cabin, looking backward down the road. He pulled his head in again, swung himself back around, and faced the dashboard. He stared coldly for a long moment, then examined the floor of the truck cabin, muttering, "I know that fuckin' bitch."

Looking into his rearview mirror, the driver caught a long-legged girl stumbling in her blue jeans and red jacket. Her boots kicked up small stones and dust. The driver down-shifted, let up on the gas, backfiring the truck, pressed his sweaty palm on the steering wheel and spun it couterclockwise from 10 to 2 o'clock. The drunk's weight pressed on his door. Afraid his passenger would fall out, the driver grabbed a handful of sweaty yellow T-shirt and yanked against the centrifugal force.

The driver straightened the wheel, ground the gears into third, saying "Fuck," and began to accelerate. The truck jumped forward, lost some of its traction on the dirt road and slid from the far right shoulder to the far left. A here-comes-a-rowdy-farm-boy cloud of brown dust billowed behind the tailgate. Irrigation ditches sat deep on either side of the road and cattails began waving from side to side in the brown air as the truck continued to gain speed.

The driver punched into fourth gear. The truck did what it had going into third. The accelerator remained flat on the floor. "Stand on the maafucker, Lyle!" the drunk hooted.

Lyle asked the drunk who the girl was. "The biggest slut in El Cajon," muttered the drunk,5 his high spirits disturbed by something. "Ya fuck her?" inquired Lyle. "Yeah, sure, once – me an' about twenty other guys."

The driver smiled to himself. He straightened his elbows back from the steering wheel, pressed his weight against the back seat and hit the brakes with one serious jolt. The drunk didn't have a chance. He had been looking at the buttons on his Levis. Completely vulnerable, he flew forward. His skull jammed into the corner where the windshield met the dashboard.

During this micro-second, he was thinking clearly. He heard the voice in his head say "dashboard." His memory provided a total recollection of his aunt's farm in Oklahoma. He hadn't seen the place in fifteen years. He remembered her grating voice whining, "Clifford, you be careful on that swing..." He could feel the warm summer wind blowing across his aunt's front yard. He could feel the gravity and release of the rope swing he was pulling against. He could see the blue sky and his little-boy knees, bare and skinned. He saw a dirty white tape bandage on his left big toe, which he held just a little bit higher than his other dirt encrusted foot, both pointing directly into the sky. He heard his aunt cough, clear her throat, and finish her warning, "...or you'll just dash your little brains out."

Clifford's head wobbled on his broken neck. His arms flapped awkwardly; a giant blood blister formed like a bruised peach over the mushy crown of his head. His ear hit the wind-wing support bar and sent blood splattering out the window and over the back of the bench seat. He shit his pants, in a single convulsive explosion; a huge volume of piss firehosed down his pantleg. His legs slid to the left along the floor, knocking Lyle's feet off the pedals. His paralyzed body flopped lengthwise on the floor.

Lyle tried frantically to kick the heavy legs off the brake and accelerator pedals. He screamed when he realized the truck was describing a slow arc with the front of the hood falling. He tried to remember the position of the wheel, but it didn't matter. The truck, in a solid bounce, crammed into the ditch on the left side of the road. Lyle's forehead sent a shower of broken glass into the air. His head popped through the pre-safety-plate glass windshield and snapped off on the bottom of the jagged hole. His head bounced once on the fender near the left headlight, right next to the spot wiped clean by the jeans of the girl he thought he loved, and had just seen in his rearview mirror for the second time this morning.

The girl paused as she noticed an abrupt end to the brown cloud of dust leading diagonally across the field to her left.

She wondered what the boys in the truck were stopping for. She shrugged and kept stumbling down the road.

BOY IN THE AIR 2

(May 3, 1964 – Balboa Stadium, San Diego)

You would have to have been in that stadium, and heard the echo every time the gun went off. You'd have to have been in the bottom, on the black asphalt with the white lines setting the limits of the lanes and the beginnings and the ends. You'd have to have been sensitive to the irony of the black surface, and the ruled white lines – and somehow linked it all with an appreciation and awe of the threat to you, and the promise to all of black athletic talent.

You'd have to have been there 25 years ago when cities ignited, fists were clenched in love and in hate, and at the same goddamn time. You'd have to have red hair, be thin with milk white skin tinted orange from the hot spring sun of this border town in the southwestern corner between the Mexican border and the blue Pacific.

You'd have to be 13 years old and dreaming of a national record in the running broad jump as they called it in those days. You'd have to be consumed with the knowledge that some kid in New Jersey had jumped 19 feet 3 inches. You'd have to accept that you were the unchallenged best jumper out of thousands of kids, except black ones, by jumping just over 17 feet. You'd listen to Keith Richards, or some other Delta blues imitator, and understand as you heard 'King Bee', that the line could be crossed in expression, but the mystery of color would never change. You'd have heard of another white rocker who just had to be named Tripp. Arnold Tripp who had been king of it all just ten years ago. Tripp the fastest boy in San Diego whose career was dumped at the state meet, when the coaches raced him on a torn hamstring – because they wanted someone to beat the niggers.

They had their Tarzan. You'd have to hate both of the words, Tarzan as much as nigger. You'd still have to bring your white skin with you to the starting line, and snort in contempt at the attitudes of both colors when the resentment came from the blacks, and racist encouragement was offered from the whites.

You'd have to be in a stadium, that echoed not only with the sound of pistol shots, but also with the sound of girls' voices high and wild with humor and sexual anticipation as they waited for Louis Rey to take his next jump. You'd have to be sitting on the grass in the blazing sun at 10:00 on a May morning looking indirectly at and listening intently to the conversation directed at a boy your own age, who came from a world with ten times the life and death of your own. Sitting there on the grass listening to the most beautiful girls in the world, gleaming white teeth, almond eyes, dark tanned deep black skin, tight skirts, white angel blouses that had heavy breasts bursting light and perfect under buttons that split and revealed black skin – and those shoes.

You'd see Louis Rey (no one ever called him just Rey, or just Louis because he was Louis Rey). Thin and muscular with large bugging eyes and a snarl for a mouth when he wasn't smiling and hair that was becoming an Afro, skin oiled to a shine and every bit the urban Masai warrior walking proud and defiant, dominant and beautiful, and better than you at what you wanted to be best at more than anything in the world. You'd watch him intently because you had enough of it yourself to know what a genius looked like, but not what one acted like, as you waited for your next jump. You'd watch the girls in the stands who were at one moment on the coolest nonchalant trip, unconcerned and casual, and the next instant spreading their legs right in the twentieth row laughing and telling Louis Rey they had something for him. Louis Rey was smiling and promising all of them a ride in his brother's car. Sharing the laugh when one of the girls asked which brother's car it would be this time since he had taken them for at least ten rides this spring in different cars and he only had three brothers. The laugh peaked when it was noted that one of his brothers was only six. Louis Rey just smiled and took his place at the end of the runway, as the entire stadium watched him. He raised his hand lightly and told the official at the take-off board, "Scratch," and jogged off across the field to talk to some older guys in trench coats with James Brown conks who seemed certain to be packing revolvers.

You'd take the lead hitting 18'10" on your next jump and there would be a spattering of applause coming from the white section high in the shade of the stadium. The announcer would declare that with one jump to go you were less than 6" from the long standing national record. You'd be wishing he never said that. You would steal a look at Louis Rey who never flinched at the announcement, but looked at the knot of white spectators as they called encouragement down to you. Ten minutes later Louis Rey would accelerate to the board, hitting an approach speed that was simply faster than you could hope to run. He'd transfer that black velocity into a neat thud and plant into a vertical lift that suspended Louis Rey in the air for a beat and another beat, and your own internal timing would be feeling your body drop because any other boy in the world would have to be dropping by now. But Louis Rey would be holding his apex because he had come in with such speed and power that he was still hovering. The stadium full of people began to sense that something was happening, but not KNOWING like you did, and the energy would cause the universal turning of a few hundred heads focusing on the boy in the air who for this instant was stopping time. Sailing above the sand, freezing your reality, taking your breath away and pissing you off in the highest sense of compliment imaginable. Gradually he wound downward and blasted the sand in a spray that surged from under his body, which bounced silently with heavy impact at a distance that was just weird. Plain weird.

"Foul," the official yelled as the red flag snapped into the air. You'd say under your breath, "Yeah, he did foul," as you jogged lightly and with more speed and spring in your legs than you ever felt before toward the hole out in the sand. It was sad, it was just the slightest foul. You'd hear your voice demanding of the official to "Measure it anyway," because you had to know. The official didn't need much prompting. Louis Rey was on the grass holding his head with tears streaming down his face, the stadium silent. Just you and the official moving in slow motion, and your voice still echoing "Measure it anyway." As they did, Louis Rey's body started shaking like he was expecting to endure a beating, and he did when he heard the official, "Jesus Christ, 22 feet, 3 inches." Louis Rey stood up and looked at you. You said, "You'll have other days Louis." Louis Rey thinking you were being mean said, "Shut up, you white motherfucker." You just stood there and said, "Nice jump anyway." He stared at you, and the girls started yelling, "Fuck him up Louis," because if they couldn't see a record they could at least hope for a fight. Louis Rey said quietly only to me, "I already did." And I smiled. And he smiled.

For George, Jackie, Miles Davis, Louis King, and the rest of us who sometimes have enough of it in ourselves to recognize it in others.

SPHINX

(August 20, 1964 – Mojave Desert)

If you were roasting in the desert, twenty-five miles from the nearest gas station, standing under the sun, shielding your eyes and watching a little dot making its way toward you, you would be struck by a major and a minor element. The major element would be the heat, and the fact that the solitary dot out there in the shimmering horizon is a junior high school boy. The minor element, the question: Why?

Pulling focus on the long lens of your imagination, you see him sweating in his shorts and T-shirt, crunching over the decomposed granite under his boots. Facing the blasting sun hanging low on the horizon, his three canteens riding the small of his back in the shade.

His boots are aptly named desert boots. They are perfect; tough tan leather, ankle high, laced in four holes on the arch to prevent hot sand and stones from falling inside, flexible thick gum soles. The boy loves those desert boots. The boots are almost the answer to our question.

Eddie feels trapped in the culture of Southern California. He is tired of the billboards offering him his own masculinity through tobaccco products. He hates the promises of confirmation of his sexuality and desirability from sports car ads on T.V. He is insulted by the assurance that he earns power and validity through the possession of this product or that, by the distorted and grotesque subliminal images promising him manhood, sex, heroism. He mistrusts the easy rites of passage supplied by his culture. He knows the commercial influences are wrong, threatening something akin to what used to be sacred.

He couldn't have put any of this into words. He feels it, with the unique clarity, and purest wisdom of adolescence. He had begun to think there was nothing he could do about it. The cultural bombardment was sneaky, constant, unavoidable. It took a gradual and relentless toll on his spirit.

Months earlier he had heard some embarrassed, uneasy laughter from his friends, and a faint voice calling him back to the school yard. "Eddie, Eddie. What the fuck, Eddie. What are ya starin' at?" He was focused on his feet, and the feet of seven of his friends all standing in a circle. Five of those friends, including Eddie, were wearing desert boots. These boots were not used in the desert, and they suddenly seemed to him part of a uniform for pretenders. If he could have taken them off his feet and thrown them into the bushes surrounding the quad he would have. Instead he stared, stunned.

He felt like a complete fraud. A fraud who hung around with other frauds, being fraudulent. He thought of a lyric from a new song by one of his favorite bands... "and he can't be a man 'cause he doesn't smoke the same cigarette as me."

The bell for class rang, scattering his friends in four directions. He lagged behind, sleepwalking his way to his math class, feeling contaminated by what a few minutes earlier had seemed like just a kids' collective sense of style. He wandered to his seat late, his face blank, unconcerned as Mrs. Fields eyed him over her glasses while marking him tardy again. His heart began pounding wildly. He understood clearly, as each thought possessed him, that he was already on his way to the desert. He stuck his feet out in the aisle and smiled.

The next weekend via Greyhound and his thumb, he was out there. He loved it. He loved it so much he kept it a secret. Once every month for the next six months, right into the teeth of summer his boots became Desert Boots. Capital D, capital B. He progressed from walking out and back in an hour or two, to elaborate treks of ten to fourteen hours, each time feeling his spirit gaining strength as he lost sight of civilization. In the last two months he started out in the dark before dawn, heading out for a point to be reached before nightfall.

The sense of accomplishment upon reaching his destination was extended and reflected upon during the ride in the Greyhound back to San Diego, prolonged during his silent, noncommittal rides as a hitchhiker from the downtown bus terminal to the eastern section of town. Waving thanks and closing the door on the stranger driving, he'd cut across orange-groved back yards and along the floors of domesticated canyons, making his way up to his front steps. He'd swing open the screen door saying, "Hi Ma, 'say Dad," and head for his bedroom.

Surging with secret pride at his accomplishment, and relishing the exhausting toll it exacted, he'd examine the dust on his boots, the sunburned skin, the burnt straw shock of hair, the salt-caked clothes. He'd open his bedroom window, take off his shorts, pull off the T-shirt and slip off those scarred, durable boots. Yanking the cool sheets back on his bed, he lay in the darkened room looking out into a world which now had boundaries no one who knew him could imagine.

He'd see the tops of the apartments sitting in the canyon that bordered his back yard. He'd listen with amused contempt to the faint calling and laughing from the miniature golf course which sat – phony and fake, unreal and gaudy – at the end of his street. The yelps and hollers would grow fainter. The sounds of the people playing and flirting on the plastic grass and trick fairways would subside entirely. His breathing would change into a slow shallow rhythm, dropping like a stone down a well into deep sleep, splashing slowly into the sweet carnal dreams of early manhood.

After these weekends he relished coming back to school, standing with his buddies in the circle, looking down at these boots and the boots of his friends and saying nothing.

There he is, a tiny dot making his seventh desert excursion, swinging along in a comfortable walking rhythm, confident that he will reach his destination. He stops, fumbles with the strap attached to the canteens, twists the top off one, and takes a long swallow. He turns an about-face in the direction from which he's come. The expanse of desert stretches flat, rippling in the growing heat. The peaks jutting in the far distance seem to Eddie as close as they appeared six hours ago. A gust of furnace wind blows over his face.

As though this were a silent signal, he turns and begins walking again. He has broken his rhythm during this forty-second stop. He will struggle out of harmony. The heat will bear down on him for several long minutes before his stride becomes the metronome that permits his mantric mindless peace. His heart palpitates at the restart. His skin flushes unbearably hot. Sweat gushes off his face. Khaki shorts find a new way to bind and hold his balls, rubbing a deeper blister between his legs.

Still in stride, he reaches into his front pocket and takes out a small sandwich bag. His fingers wiggle in the plastic and remove a melted glob of Vaseline. His hand slips under his waistband. He stops, spreads his legs, and smears the goo around his crotch. The boots crunch along once again, searching for the harmonic drum of his steps on the desert floor. The heat has swollen his penis. He feels awkward as it flexes and flops until it finds its spot, riding the rhythm between the hot wet shorts and his bare Vaselined leg.

He begins to think of his best friend's mother down the street. Beautiful, warm disposition, a light, insightful sense of humor. He imagines her flat-roofed stucco tract home. He sees her on her couch. Lying on her side in the dark with the curtains pulled against the afternoon sun. He sees her ankles crossed and her body stretched out. Her palm is resting behind her sweating neck, revealing a black patch of armpit next to her face. Her breasts are outlined in the transparent, sweat-soaked, white cotton blouse. She slowly lifts her hips and shifts her weight toward the outside of the couch. Her eyes are closed. She's nearly asleep, wide-hipped, heavy-breasted, peaceful.

The fan, which always sits on the parquet floor during hot weather, buzzes left to right, an admiring machine repeating its once-over from head to toe. Repeating toe to head, head to toe, over and over. The breeze hits her thighs, flowing up the stream of her loose dress, following the indented line to the V under her stomach, fluttering her dress, trembling in the V, and continuing. It buzzes over the stomach, up along her breasts, giving her nipples a pulsation of cool against the white wet cloth, causing a slight blush and tightness.

The fan continues up the curves of her thin muscular neck and stops on her beautiful face to reverse direction. A few sweat-joined strands of jet-black hair reverberate along her cheek for a second. Asleep. Her face turns like a dark flower to the cool moon of the fan's breeze. Her lips kiss the fan's invisible pressure, her tongue sliding slowly along her upper lip, pulling cool drops of sweat into her mouth. The fan's buzz changes to a deeper tone and travels down her body.

Eddie stumbles, unconscious of the variation of his cadence, on and on, over and around the knee-high brush, zig-zagging along the frying desert floor. "Where am I? I'm here and I'm OK... still have a canteen and a half of water... about four or five hours to the gas station... it's only... 4:30... shit... but,... hell, the headlights on the road work pretty good... like last time... full moon up at 8... plenty of time... I'm not scared, am I?" His heart pounds slightly. He swallows and waits for panic. Nothing. "No." He checks his bearings, tuning in a slow circle, finding all the landmarks exactly where he wants them to be. "Four-thirty-two..four or five hours..." His heart races. He inhales the hot air deeply, blows it out and inhales again blows it out fast and inhales again.

"Fuck that. Who the fuck cares what time it is or what the fuck time I get there?... I got the fucking direction and I don't need to waste my fucking energy getting all the fuck worked up over fucking nothing. Fuck it. I ain't scared and I'm not to start getting fucking scared by wondering what the fuck time it is, or when the fuck I'm getting where the fuck I'm going." You'd have heard him laughing at himself if you had happened to be in the middle of the Mojave in August 1964. "I'm not scared, I'm Ok. Now where was I? Oh, yeah."

He sees her again. It was the time he came to her house last week. It was really hot that day. Good thing he wasn't out here then, 106 in San Diego. That'd be somewhere like 120 out here. Anyway, he went into her house in the late afternoon. The house was asleep, everything completely still. He trailed the absence of sound out to the back yard patio, found the woman's husband and their kids passed out in the heat, lying on mattresses they had dragged outside into the shade.

He could hear pipes and faucets sputter from the bathroom shower inside the house, settling into a high-pressure rain. The woman gasped for breath as she stepped into the shower. He argued with himself as he involuntarily walked back into the house. His silent steps wound from the patio along the corridor between the bedrooms and the bathroom. From the amplified splash and the sound of the spray and the bare feet squeaking against the wet porcelain, he determined that the bathroom door remained wide open. He could hear the water storming over her body and exploding in wet impact on the floor of the tub. Taking a breath, he turned the corner of the corridor and faced the bathroom. Cold steamless water ran over her silhouette, streams of water raced in clear webs on the inside of the shower curtain. The shadow bent at the waist and long arms stretched downward, breasts falling easily under shoulders, head down, hair hanging like a black waterfall.

She stood up, arms pulling the mane of hair up and over her shoulders. Her face was tilted upward, her mouth open. The jet of water blasting against her neck. Cool air swirled from the bathroom door.

She twisted the faucet shut. Eddie slipped out of the doorway and waited. Hearing her yank the shower curtain aside, he timed his voice to say, "Robert?.." with perfect innocence, and turned the corner. Her eyes met his. She was mid-stride, one leg suspended over the rim of the tub. She made no effort to cover herself, but froze there like a photograph, her eyes driving into his, betraying a mixture of curiosity and amusement.

She stood there, skin gleaming, holding his eyes prisoner with a magnetic power within her gaze. He could see nothing of her but a terrifying and increasing depth behind her eyes. He felt his body go weightless in panic as he realized he was far beyond his depth.

At that instant she smiled and reached smoothly for a towel and hugged it front of herself. She glanced out of the side of her eye, letting slip for an instant something that felt to Eddie like understanding and forgiveness, unsettling him even more and informing him immediately who held all the power. Her attitude shamed him, as though in these frozen instants he could see the real meaning of his mistake.

It was as though she had expected, even recognized, the inevitability of this contact but was disappointed in what Eddie had done with it. Without a word, she told him he had gone about it entirely wrong, and although she would not use the word, he knew "fool" was the only one appropriate. His face burned, his eyes dropped down, unfocused. Still holding her image, almost but not quite registering his boots on the wooden floor, he said, "Oh, I'm sorry."

Her voice held a curious tone, coming from deeper in her chest, ironic and more real than it had ever sounded to him before. It made him imagine the way she would sound giving simple directions to a stranger who had lost his way. A matter-of-fact voice that in some way labeled him an equal. It seemed final and strangely welcome, spoken under her breath. A code, a frightening challenge, a whispered riddle. "Oh, yeah, sure, you are."

SHERRY BABY

(July 25, 1964 – San Diego, California)

Eleven-thirty, a moonless night. Empty streets in suburbia. The tenth day of a heat wave. The Santana gusts hot and dry, ninety-two degrees. Eddie Burnett is urinating under a street lamp on the middle of an asphalt road. It is a tradition with him this summer. Standing in one spot, he turns a slow circle. His record is four revolutions. He calls them "piss rings." He does this almost every night on the way home from his girlfriend's house. The rings stain the road for several days. Each night a new overlapping ring, until he gets five. He is doing this to commemorate the 1964 Summer Olympic Games.

His girlfriend's house? Not really. That is, it is an unrequited love. Sherry likes him, but on the social level he is considered much too goony for her. Eddie does not quite get it. He gets his hair cut by his mother, and dresses from the Navy PX, with no sense of style and, worse, no interest in it. The social situation means much less to Sherry than the sense that Eddie doesn't trust something about himself. She puzzles at his obvious feeling of inferiority, despite qualities that should make him confident. She wishes Eddie would find that place which gives most of the other boys the ground they stand on. He seems to have lost that place, or had it stolen. Sherry's curiosity and attraction comes from the feeling that Eddie knows where that place is, needs it, and thinks it is worthless at the same time. He speaks in a code, using images that create unwholesome feelings in Sherry. They appeal to something essential inside of herself that she fears most. Just about everything he has to say makes Sherry laugh, or seems faintly intimidating, as though he knew some bitter secret.

Eddie is especially happy tonight, though. Earlier today Sherry passed her Coke bottle to him. When he passed it back, she just finished it off without a second glance. Right in front of her friends. Didn't check for backwash or anything. Didn't even wipe the lip of the bottle. To Eddie and to the other kids, this gesture spoke of intimacy.

Sherry's hair is summer blond, her eyes are gray. She smells stunningly innocent. She's ripe and it's all operating, pulsating just under the surface. Eddie is in full-throttle, aching adolescent love.

Mornings they meet at the beach. She rides with a girlfriend's mother or older brother. Eddie thumbs out with a couple of the guys, making a heroic beach entrance from the far reaches of thirty miles of inland freeway.

Sherry knows she drives them all crazy. She sees it as their problem and has zero patience with any boy who brings it up. The boys her own age can speak of almost nothing else in the minutes that follow seeing her. Men pull over in their cars to holler their promises to her. She sends them off stammering insults in her general direction, with about the same effect on Sherry as if they were bouncing off a nearby lamp post. Nothing disturbs her self-possession. For this quality Eddie adores her. Her beauty is only secondary.

He is fascinated to discover that her self-possession is not the result of insensitivity or a callous stupidity, but is fueled by her tremendous intelligence and fierce courage.

Tonight; as Eddie finishes off the last piss ring, he hears Sherry's voice from the phone call that afternoon. Minutes earlier he had been in her front room keeping her company as she ironed clothes for the entire family. He hears her soft, trusting voice as she sobs tearful-hateful-father misunderstandings. Sherry is being punished for being out too late the night before with Eddie, and for coming home with grass stains on her white shorts.

Eddie had walked her home. They were only a few minutes late. He made her laugh at something. There was an intoxicating jasmine bush hovering over their heads. Suddenly a wrestling match exploded. Sherry and Eddie struggled against each other on the warm, wet lawn. A blue light shined out of the window of some stranger's house as they sat inside watching Ed Sullivan on T.V.

When Sherry's father inevitably forbade her to see Eddie, he spent his nights, wings clipped, perched on the rims of the canyons of his childhood, looking down into an expanse of darkness.

He had already lost his direction. That summer he didn't go to movies, or hang out with his friends. He didn't go to the beach, or read, or learn to do anything new. He was overwhelmed. He needed Sherry.

He dragged around the streets at night, trying to dodge the ultraconservative, ultramilitary San Diego police department. Eddie had already been introduced to the San Diego police. It had occurred on a sidewalk two summers earlier.

Cops pull up in their cruiser. Cops jump out. Cops tell Eddie to stand still. Cops throw him facedown, pin his arms, shove his face into the concrete, twist his wrists, ratchet on the cuffs. Cops throw him in the cruiser, banging his head into the door jam as they toss him into the back seat. They drive him someplace, and tell him to get out. They walk him to a screen door, where a woman with a purple swollen face and a bloody cloth held over her mouth says, "No, that's not him."

Cops take off the handcuffs. They try to tell Eddie they are sorry, but add that he "...answered the lady's description." Eddie looks at the short red-headed one, with stubble like rust on his chin. Immediately Eddie understands something about the genetics of outlaws. He senses something that is not in his favor, in fact quite the opposite. It's as though from that moment on, he saw the line drawn in front of his feet. Something they think makes him wrong; and he knows makes him right. He looks at the cop and smiles, "That's alright, I'll always answer the description." The rusty face contorts at an equation, the face cannot find the sum. The cop takes his stand behind authority: his weight settles on his spread feet, his pelvis shifts forward and this conversation is over. The other cop offers Eddie a ride home. He looks like his feelings are hurt when Eddie replies, "No, thanks."

After that initial meeting, it seemed the cops felt that they should find something he had done to justify their mistake. They picked him up and drove him home alot. Parked squad car rumbling in front of his house, neighbors opening curtains watching his parents' place.

In response, Eddie committed as much malicious mischief as he possibly could for the next year and a half. Specifically motivated in his contest with the cops, generally motivated by the silent, stucco, lawn-sprinkler existence of San Diego. The contest was a tie. Eddie didn't get caught, but he remained stuck within the quiet, soulless, white- pebbled roofs, all contained by the cops. But by the time he met, and lost, Sherry, he was leaving the community alone, and wasting his time by himself.

Sherry was in a car with her big brother and one of his friends. Eddie was on foot carrying a couple bags of groceries home. He felt something was wrong before he turned around to see the smirking faces on the boys, and heard the enthusiastic shouting of his name called out of the car window. He managed an awkward acknowledging jerk of his head above the bags in the general direction of Sherry as she passed out of sight, sitting in the front seat between two football heroes.

He finally dropped the bags on the kitchen table and said, "I'm taking a walk" to his mother, who tried to stop him but gave up as the screen door swung closed.

She may have only wondered why Eddie would want to take a walk in 102-degree heat immediately after carrying two full bags of groceries a half mile. Maybe she wanted to offer him an iced coffee, or ask him why he got in so late last night, or would Sherry like to come to dinner some night, and she hadn't seen much of Sherry lately… was anything wrong?

Eddie was walking in the dehydrating, asphalt-melting, cornea-frying, lip-cracking summer weather of interior San

Diego. His head ached, it buzzed with fatigue. He made himself go look at the tire tracks on the shoulder of the road leading from Food Basket. He was slouched more than ever, his face parallel to the mushy black road. He was not moving across the busy intersection fast enough for the man driving the station wagon.

Eddie is in the middle of the crosswalk, directly in front of the station wagon's two-tone baby-shit-brown hood. He can smell the suffering fan belt's burning skin. He hears the wheezing radiator. The windshield reflects a blinding glare. HONK! HONK! HOOOONNNNKKK! Eddie is stunned. He stands there, then turns and faces the guy driving, who emanates a tremendous amount of loathing. He starts to walk again. HOOOO-ONNNNNNKKKKK!

Eddie gets to the far right headlight and turns an about-face, crossing the front of the hood again. The man starts yelling shit at Eddie. He sticks his American-man war-hero head out of his car and spews more shit at him. Eddie makes another about-face and crosses in front of the car again. The door swings open. The man clomps his backache out of the seat. His hard soles hit the pavement; his sweaty shirt is stuck to his pear-shaped body. He swaggers toward Eddie with balled fists.

Eddie is supposed to run. But he is pissed. The man grabs for the boy's T-shirt and tries to stretch it within the grasp of his other hand. Eddie cannot believe that this fat fuck thinks he is going to treat him like a child. It seems almost funny that the man thinks he can yell and try to overpower him with his adult-size bulk. Eddie jerks loose of the man's awkward grabbing. The man's fingernails tear into Eddie's arm. In an instant, Eddie has hit him – hard. The shot is planted on the side of the man's crew-cut. The man is already tilted downward, from just that one quick pop. Disgusted, Eddie belts him again. The man hits the pavement. Eddie leans down, lines up the spot where the jaw line meets the neck under the ear, and passes. Blam, he hits him in the forehead. Just because the man doesn't have basic respect for anyone; because he honks at barefoot kids in hot crosswalks going too slow. He honks, honks, honks, at disillusioned, nothing-to-live-for, nothing-to-die-for-kids. He puts his hands on people he doesn't know. The man wants to intimidate other people, too busy ignoring his own kids, who are staring at Eddie in terror.

Daddy's kids are crying. Boy, are they crying. Screaming. Daddy is lying on the ground trying to get his burning elbows off the furnace-hot grit. Daddy is flopping around with his equilibrium fucked up from the knots on his head. The kids are under 10, two little girls and the youngest a boy. They keep repeating, "Daddy, Daddy, Daddy," in sobbing, breathless screams. Eddie has a vacant feeling, as though there is nothing left of himself. If he'd put it in words, it would have had something to do with nature, what he had done, and the way he felt about those kids felt unnatural.

The wife is sitting in the honey seat. While Dear is getting up on his knees, Eddie sees the wife's wide eyes. He knows that he has humiliated her husband. Her desperate expression tells Eddie that he has given her husband problems he will not overcome, and those problems will extend to her and her innocent kids. That although she will never express anything but hatred to Eddie, at the same moment she is pleading with him to do something. It is his responsibility because he is the one standing. Eddie's remorse at the sound of the shrieking children, and the sexual tilt in the woman's unspoken plea, is more than he can handle this morning. Eddie walks over to the curb and sits down. He realizes the man's behavior is not an isolated incident, and his wife probably hates him as much as Eddie does. But the kids.

Dear staggers to the car and parks it across the street. He's yelling brave things now, since it is apparent Eddie is down for the count. The blustering pear is just that kind of guy. Then Honey starts yelling about the police and runs into Speedee Mart.

The stock boy, a friend from elementary school, comes running out in his green apron. He squats down next to Eddie on one knee, surveying the commotion building on the corner.

"You better get the hell outta here, Eddie. They already called the cops." Eddie mumbles, "That's good." He focuses on a gum wrapper between his dirty, calloused feet. His heart is exploding in fear and anger. The fear is climbing and the anger is falling. He wishes they would just drive away. He knows they won't.

The cops come. Dear stands there, the center of self-righteous attention. The cops stand nearby, regarding Eddie like a rabid dog. Eddie overhears Honey, who evidently has read Newsweek, because she is certain that Eddie is on "pot" or he would have run away. Dear picks up his cue and makes it clear in a loud voice to all the bystanders that people on "pot" have more strength than normal, and that is the reason he didn't kick the kid's butt. They start speaking in quiet voices suggesting that Eddie is winding down from some high and is falling into a stupor. The kids have quieted down. Eddie sits there smelling the wrapper. He'd bet it was Juicy Fruit – wrong, it was spearmint. Slight smile in the corner of Eddie's mouth. Sentence inside his head – "Just not my day." The man stands next to the big guys with the guns, nodding his head in some social bond. Eddie looks at Honey, who is smug with the knowledge that she has, probably for the thousandth time, gotten Dear his balls back.

But as the black and white pulls away with a silent Eddie in the back seat, it's because Eddie wants the kids to see the police take the bad guy away.

BUCEPHALUS

(September 5, 1964 – San Diego, California)

I was fifteen. I'd just gotten out of Juvy, and my parents were pretty upset. I was starting my first year in high school and I was hoping to do something right. My father told me I was trying out for the school football team. As usual, I wasn't in a position to argue with him. I knew I'd never make the team anyway. So there I was on September 5, 1964, at 9:30 a.m., sitting in the locker room of Wilson High School, the pride of Interscholastic sports in San Diego, California.

I had a helmet that didn't fit right, way too loose. It looked stupid. My neck was too thin, my eyes too big, my face to narrow. The idea of intimidating anyone in the locker room was laughable. I sat in front of my locker with tunnel vision. Putting on the gear I was having an anxiety attack, before I ever got near the football field. I sat there surrounded by last year's championship players, thinking, "Dad would just love this." The linemen were acting big and brutish, defensive linemen especially. The linebackers were the characteristic psychopaths everyone imagines linebackers to be. There was a cluster of pretty-boy stars, undoubtedly the quarterbacks, running backs and receivers. They were all smiling, telling jokes, happy to have another year of glory, admiration, and sex beginning again.

I sat there in my underwear and socks with the huge helmet wobbling on my head, a ridiculous stranger. These other guys looked like giants; thick cords ran up and down their wide brown necks. Whiskers collected beads of sweat. They looked at me kind've funny. Each pair of eyes would dart at me; each pair assessed me as nothing – that bugged me. I lifted the helmet off my head and put it on the floor as nonchalantly as possible – I had noticed that no one else was wearing his. I reached down for one of my cleated football shoes. At that instant, a huge foot sent it spinning along the concrete floor. I got so nervous I nearly fainted. My brain struggled frantically to determine if this was intentional or accidental. What challenge or warning should I declare? How could I get out of this without looking more absurd than I felt, which was very absurd? Without looking up, I crouched down, staring at the floor, and stretched a few small steps, reaching for my shoe. I could see a thousand tails on a thousand dogs tucked under a thousand chicken-shit dog butts.

A thick-wristed hand intercepted the shoe and handed it back, saying, "Sorry, Red, here ya go." "Thanks," I peeped without looking up. Red. I hated to be called Red. This guy didn't know my name, sees my red hair, red freckles, red nose, and assumes my fucking name is Red. Plus, I knew that if he had intentionally kicked my shoe again, I would have chickened out.

I hid my burning face and pretended to need something in my locker. I dove way in, smelling at least eight years of athletic tradition at Wilson High School. My thoughts echoed, "This is not a good start."

My father never taught me a thing. He hardly ever said anything to me. He never put his hand on my shoulder, never extended it in a handshake, never even slapped me with it. He saved that for my mother. It was clear that he thought I didn't exist, wasn't even worth the bother.

He was a hero. He was compromised by his war experiences, but he still walked with the stride of a leader of men. He drank too much, and he was pretty fucked up when I was younger. He was a sergeant-at-arms with cannon-ball biceps. He used an "Aw-shucks" style of humor that stung like hell but was really funny anyway. He was always making me laugh and hurting me at the same time. He had rock-a-billy hair and sloped powerful shoulders, stood six-foot four, and smelled sort of randy with smoke and beer. He always got smiles from the women that knew him, and furtive glances and a smile from any who didn't. He accepted this as his due and kept walking. He never walked next to me or my mother. He had an old M-1 in his closet with a chunk kicked out of the stock near the grip where an Italian's bullet had ricocheted. He had a glass eye. He cracked his knuckles, belched his beer and watched lots of football on T.V., and was drunk all the time.

We were going into the second hour of tryouts. The grass was shining. The ground was soft; the sprinklers had been on early that morning. The sun shone with surreal heat directly above. We'd heard speeches from coaches and listened to stars of last year's team urging us to win again. With the team in a tight knot in the center of the field, upperclassmen were impressing younger boys with references to parties and dances that followed last season's games – the emphasis was on "pussy." I looked at my feet. I'd never so much as held a girl's hand. The father of the only girl I had a chance with wouldn't let me see her. I began to hate these stars with their girlfriends, their own cars and their friends to eat lunch with.

The sidelines were deep with kids. Several parents walked up and down talking easily, fathers with chests expanded in vicarious pride. A ring of girls stood on the thirty-yard line. They were dressed casual, in revealing hot-weather clothes; they had tanned silky skin. They seemed to be having a subliminal conversation from the waist down with some of the older boys, secretive and tentative. As far as I could tell, this looked like the big time.

We'd been told that we were going to close out the practice with "contact drills." I had heard "men from boys muttered at least twenty times in reference to these contact drills. We had been racing each other by positions earlier, and I had always been pretty fast. The stars from last year's team seemed a little upset when I kept winning the races. Some of the guys were friendly about it, but they already knew they were slow. The ones that thought they were fast were pissed. I knew the coaches liked speed, and they began to pay more attention to me. The stars didn't like that much, either. I felt the tide turning against me.

A fat red-faced coach screamed, "ALRIGHT – on the thirty YARD LINE." The two stars beside me started making television-sounding war cries. I got disgusted and jogged over to where they were lining up. This is what they had been waiting for. I noticed, how much bigger the other players were. I also noticed the pairs of eyes that stared at me, and the knots of players looking my direction and talking quietly among themselves. A coach came over and asked me what position I was trying out for. I just said, "defense." Two guys made derisive sounds. I looked at them; they looked at me. I didn't like them; they didn't like me.

Two days earlier I had been sitting in the front room with my dad, the curtains drawn. He was watching a team from his home state of Texas playing the rival state, Oklahoma. My mother came from Oklahoma. As a result, she was subjected to merciless teasing from my dad. Especially when he'd been drinking. We were the Okies. I was born in El Paso. He was born north and a hell of a lot closer to Oklahoma than I was, but to him I was the "goddamn Okie."

There he was, sitting in the dark watching the football game – silent, emotionless, intent. His hips and back would jump involuntarily as he watched the athletes smashing into each other. He popped numerous beers, which were in a neat row beside the lazy-boy chair and were removed silently by my mother at odd intervals.

I sat down in a chair near him, watching him and hoping he would want to talk to me about trying out for the team. He was a big star halfback in high school. Trophies, scrap books, the whole bit. I didn't care if he got drunk and told me about his five-touchdown night again. But he didn't say anything. The game on T.V. was pretty good. The lead changed hands several times, the players were making great runs, the hitting was vicious. Sometimes the camera would pan the stadium packed with delirium and pretty girls. Oklahoma won. Dad stood up and glared at me, spun a tight circle, sat back down and said, "Goddamn it, goddamn Okies, everyone of 'em halfbreed morons."

They started interviewing Number 43 from Oklahoma. When the kid said where he lived, my dad said, "Just down the road from your mother." The T.V. showed three plays the kid made; an incredible run with an interception and two hits near the goal line on the Texas halfback that had my dad saying, "Oh, man." The Oklahoma coach put his arm over the shoulder of Number 43, who looked like he was in elementary school, kinda skinny, with a big ol' grin. The coach said a couple of nice things about all the players on his team and then, referring to the kid who was now dodging a few towels his teammates were throwing at him because he was on T.V., said, "It ain't the size of the dog in the fight, it's the size of the fight in the dog."

My dad looked over at me, and his hand switched off the T.V. "Didja hear that? Truer words were never spoken." Then he walked out to the front yard. I didn't follow him. I went down the street to see some friends who came from Texas and Oklahoma too and were proud of it. I tried out the thing the coach said on the boys and it went over with them like a new motto.

I was pulling off my jersey, it was stuck to my pads with sweat. I was grass-stained, scraped up and laughing to myself because I couldn't believe how good I felt. Every time I lined up for my turn during the contact drills I could hear my father, "Didja hear that...?" I'd watch the players' faces as they came swaggering up to the line and I saw that look change to fear the next time. I saw many faces alter and self-doubt cloud innocent eyes. I kept feeling an impact on them that they obviously knew nothing about. Before too long they were trying to protect themselves instead of trying to run over me. That made it worse for them. I just did what I was supposed to do, like I'd seen the kid do on T.V. In the locker room I kept how I felt to myself. I wasn't saying anything to anyone. I wasn't putting my head in my locker either.

Someone I didn't know was helping me out of my jersey; when I turned to thank him, he was gone. My eyes searched the room, and any eyes that met mine looked down at the floor. I wanted to ask them what they were afraid of, but I knew it would be a long season, and in a few weeks they would see me as a teammate instead of someone who was going to knock their dicks in the dirt every practice.

The red-faced coach yelled out the practice times for tomorrow's tryouts. Then he looked at me. "Way to go out there, Red. Where do you come from ?"

I said, "Oklahoma."

BEST TIME OF THE DAY

(September 21, 1964 – San Diego, California)

The hot air is building outside of Wanda Monroe's house. Inside, the hint of a breeze flows in drafts over the living room's parquet floor, carrying with it the smell of Bruce's floor wax, and causing the dust mice under the furniture to swirl in silent tiny tornados. A Gibson is leaning in one corner of the room. A television is surrounded by a couch, a worn Lazyboy and a rocking chair. Behind the couch is a large dining table with mix-matched chairs: two aluminum, one wooden, a couple of stools and a broken high chair.

Sitting on the table are condiments: salt and pepper shakers, mustard and ketchup squeeze bottles, a large pour-type sugar container and a paper napkin dispenser. Everything that you would find in an all-night roadside diner. The floor is littered with newspapers. On a coffee table nearest the couch rests an empty cereal bowl beside a huge ashtray heaped with butts. A dusty old fan sits in one corner. On the floor beside the rocking chair, an ancient Zenith radio buzzes.

Wanda Monroe walks into the living room and stops, looking out the screen door into the twilight. Her hair is thick and black, shoulder length. Her eyes are also black, her skin is brown, her lips full. She has wide full hips, a narrow waist, long muscular legs, huge hands, and firm breasts that have weight. She is a 35-year-old exhausted mother of five. Her hands are pressed into the small of her back. She emits a slight groan as her pelvis sways forward. Tentatively one hand rises to her face until one long finger sweeps the sweat from her forehead and flicks the drops onto the tiny squares of the screen. She stares from out of the door, her eyes losing focus. Slowly the hands that seem to have a purpose of their own in their slow and constant movements press into her back again. Her eyes clear for a second. Timed with the slow tilting of her head they again lose focus and stare into the floor. The hand lifts slowly to her lips, her little finger flicks like a slow switch-blade, and the long sharp nail traces the indentation between her bicuspid and an incisor. She stares out, wondering for the ten thousandth time how she got here. In this early transition into night, the years from her youth and the present become blurred. She closes her eyes and listens to the voices in the neighborhood, calling children home for dinner or delaying a request in the interest of some other chore. "...I'll be there in a second... I've just got this last section to wax." Calls back and forth across the street. "Janet, is Jack over there ?" "No, he and Eddie and the dogs were heading for the canyon last I saw them. That was about two hours ago." "If you see them, tell Jack that his dinner is cold. Hey – oh, never mind, I'll tell you tomorrow."

Wanda can listen and hear her own mother calling her from a time when she was a lot happier and a lot less lonely back in Oklahoma. Her eyes closed, Wanda calls up all the sights of the street she grew up on. Darkness sets on that remembered street and she sees the headlights of her older brother's Plymouth jumping down the road leading to their home. She sees the face of her brother's best friend asking her if she didn't want to come along with them into town. Her heart hammers inside her chest. She hears her brother's friend urging her, "Yeah, Wanda c'mon. We'll let ya sing." How she had felt herself split in two, a scared shy daughter, fearful of the mere idea of going into a place like that, and the other side thinking, "Shit yeah, I'll sing alright, I'll sing until you won't ever hear anything else... but my singing." She went. She had her first husband three months later, her first child six months after that. Rock-a-bye baby. Wanda heard the voices inside of the liquor store, she remembered the look in his eyes when he came running out, heard herself saying.."Oh, my God no." She saw the gun in his hand, and his laughing face. Saw her brother stumble over the confused farmer in the doorway. Heard the car doors slam after the tires had already begun screeching. Felt his hands press her onto the floor of the backseat and heard her brother saying... "Get down, Lyle, here it comes." She remembered the muffled explosions and the sound like a beer opener popping into the trunk of the car. She remembered the kiss he gave her when they crossed the state line and he whispered "Welcome to the Lone Star State." She knew right then and there she'd never see her mother again.

The buzzing radio annoys her. She walks over to the rocking chair, slumps into its cushions and adjusts the radio to the top-40, hoping to hear Brenda Lee. Instead, the weather report, "Expect temperatures to increase over the next three days as the seasonal Santana winds are expected to drive temperatures above 100 degrees." Something makes her laugh her frequent good-natured chuckle, and the fingers of her hands pull through her long hair.

Eddie Burnett knocks softly against the screen door with one knuckle. Before Wanda can reply, he walks into the room. The knocking serves as a formality, giving him permission to proceed as though he were one of the family. Which in nearly every respect he is, and has been since he was seven years old. Eddie is wearing black pointed shoes with white socks, Levis and a poorly ironed button-down shirt. His hair is not behaving. Instead of the sleek order it held for a few seconds as he left the bathroom mirror, it has reverted to an explosion of orange haystack. Eddie seems mildly concerned with this condition and attempts to plaster it into some sort of part, but each gesture becomes increasingly half-hearted.

"Hey, Wanda."

"Hi, Eddie."

"Boys here ?"

"Nobody's here."

"Oh."

Eddie sits down on the couch, passing up the Cosmopolitan

for a Saturday Evening Post. He is feeling absolutely confused. Normally he would be saying, "Uh, see ya." and be out the screen door. He finds himself sitting here in the front room with Wanda and nobody else home. He looks at the Cosmopolitan.

"Shucks, I was hopin' to get a ride to the game. Don't matter though, really."

Eddie pauses for a few seconds and blurts out a comment that surprises him.

"I'm not ready to play tonight. It's just..."

Wanda leans back into the chair and crosses her feet on the coffee table. Her loose cotton dress slips up her leg for an instant, and she gently pulls it over her knee. She sees the breath catch in Eddie's chest. It surprises her when she deliberatly readjusts her feet and allows the dress to slip up her leg again. Eddie pinches a nostril with his thumb and forefinger, his eye darting in her direction. His neck feels funny. What was he saying ?

"Well, Eddie... the boys tell me you've been just tearin' it up in practice. Don't tell them I told you."

Eddie knows the boys would never acknowledge their admiration to his face but inside it makes him feel great, just thinking of them telling Wanda of his exploits. He thought he sensed a feeling of pride in them when they sat together at lunch even though the guys on the team and even some seniors saved him a place. But hell, what could he talk about with those guys? And the Monroe boys, well, they know more about what is really happening than any of those snobs, anyway.

"That's not what I mean. I mean, yeah, sure I can play and all – and I want to play. But..."

Wanda is feeling more than the normal tension in Eddie tonight. She thinks she can recognize the feeling – something from her memory. It bothers her.

"They just now left."

"Well, maybe I'll walk. Don't want to ask my Dad. He's going to the game."

She looks at Eddie as he cracks his knuckles. So that's it. I don't blame him. Wanda shudders at the thought of Eddie's father hooting his drunken head off in front of a few thousand PTA types. It surprises Wanda that Eddie's father could actually get it together to leave the house and arrive anyplace.

"Really ?"

"Yeah, saw him with Buster and his moron brother coming out of the liquor store, hollering about seeing me tonight."

Eddie tells himself that he doesn't care what his father does. Everyone is going to find out what he's like sooner or later anyway. But he doesn't believe himself. He feels trapped. Maybe he – ah, hell, he has to play. What would he say to the coaches?

"He's proud of you Eddie."

"Yeah, he thinks he's playin'… uh, can I use the phone?

"Sure."

Eddie dials home.

"Hey, Ma. Dad there? Oh. So how ya doin'? No. I'm not excited… The boys – yeah, was gonna get a ride. Naw, don't worry about it. He was? Yeah, I know. It's ok. How 'bout you? Ok. I'll be back late. Sherry's. No, now that I'm playin' her dad loves me. Yeah, her too. Milk and cookies, the whole nine yards. Weird, huh? He's with Buster, I guess. I'll call ya from Sherry's. Yeah. Yeah, we'll win. Both. Defense and offense. No. It's better. If I thought I was gonna get hurt I wouldn't be playin', Ma. Don't worry. He'll be alright. Yeah, sure. Thanks, Ma. See ya in the morning. I will. Bye."

Wanda has been watching Eddie intently. She cannot see anything about him that should make him an unusual athlete. He's kinda skinny in fact. There is something inside that has always been there, and although he could get a little out of control sometimes, it didn't seem to be anything he could use. He wasn't as tough as her sons. Not even close. But her sons wouldn't mess with Eddie either. The kid had a crazy streak. But he didn't get it from his mother or father. Unless… his father. No. He wasn't like his dad. Took after his mother, sorta. She felt so strange when she asked herself, "I wonder what this boy is gonna be like in bed?" It was a direction she didn't want to go. But as soon as she'd thought it, she knew it was the direction she was going. She knew it was the direction she had been going for the last few months, maybe couple of years even if she didn't want to admit it.

In the next instant she saw herself getting into her brother's car on the way to town to sing. She heard the farm boys hollering again for another song. She remembered the way she felt. How it had been the best feeling, and the most dreadful feeling at the same time. How late that night beneath the trees next door she had spread out the blanket stolen from her sleeping house with a final sense of determination to make sure the feelings from that stage would last up inside of her until morning. And they had, and then some. She didn't think she would like it, but she did. She was as good at it as she was at singing. Almost like there was no difference. Just take a deep breath and let what was going to happen, happen. Just find the power you're born with, and then stay out of the way. She knew when she felt his body stretching into a hard panting straining animal that he was going to let loose inside her. And she didn't care. And she cried at the knowledge that she didn't care, that she had finally left herself behind. And become something else. A woman. It was time. That's all. It didn't turn out so bad. She looked at Eddie.

"Eddie, the boys were telling me this morning that you could jump across this room."

"How big's the room?"

"I don't know."

Eddie stands against the far wall and begins counting, measuring one foot in front of the other.

"I find this a little hard to believe."

Eddie stops and looks up saying, "I get a running start."

"Well, yes. I know that Eddie. I didn't think you were from Mars."

"Oklahoma."

"I thought you were born in El Paso."

"I was, but that's not where I come from."

"What does he mean by that?" thought Wanda.

"15... 16... 17... 18..."

"What'd ya jump?"

"Twenty-one feet."

"19... 20... 21... Yeah, guess so."

Eddie looked at Wanda and tried not to be reminded of Sherry when he caught the look on Wanda's face. He refused to believe that the look was nearly the same as the look Sherry had just before she pulled him close to her. He knew it was the same look.

"Looks pretty far in here. Kinda hard for me to believe, too." He noticed that his voice had a strange quivering sound around its edges. Wanda started to get up with an empty coffee cup.

"Another kid jumped 22. Here, I'll get it." Eddie takes the empty coffee cup and walks into the kitchen. Wanda calls over her shoulder to Eddie, who rattles the coffee pot on the stove and runs fresh water from the sink.

"The boys are going to the beach tomorrow, you going?"

"Yeah, storm surf – huge. Still 'red tide,' though."

Red tide, thought Wanda. "What's red tide ?"

"I dunno – some kinda plankton, I think. Makes the water smell kinda funny. It gets dark-colored. When you get out you feel sticky. Most people don't like it. At night when the surf breaks, it shines. It glows in the dark. Really beautiful."

"Never heard of it. Glows in the dark?"

"Yep."

Wanda saw Eddie standing at the foot of her bed glowing in the dark, and the blood on her skin and blanket under the tree in Oklahoma.

"If you don't get going, you're gonna miss the game. Sherry'll be fit to be tied."

Eddie returns to the living room and stands behind Wanda. He is thinking of Sherry's father and his own father sitting there in the stands cheering away. He wishes they would outlaw parents at these games. If she could, though, he'd like his mother to come. But that would be too much. His father only acts worse when she's there.

"I wish it was just a game, not this big show. It just doesn't matter. Even Sherry doesn't get it. She always wants me to see things like everyone else. Sometimes I get sick of Sherry."

"Really, I thought you guys were in love."

Wanda draws out "in love" in a Gomer Pyle imitation. When she sees Eddie's expression she drops the teasing and states seriously, "The boys say you're crazy about her, and I think she's real cute... sweet."

"That's right. She is. Perfect."

"That's not what I meant and you know it." Wanda couldn't miss the sense of frustration in Eddie's voice. Wanda knows Sherry comes from a family that aspires to be above the rest of the neighborhood. She's always thought it romantic that Sherry and Eddie were together. It seemed so natural and so absolutely wrong at the same time.

"Her father kicked me out of the house two weeks ago. Tonight he's my best friend."

"Well, I've kicked you out of my house a couple times as I remember and tonight I'm your best friend."

"It's different."

"How?"

"It just is.."

"Eddie, we're all just people you know."

"What do you mean?"

"We're fallible. Sometimes, we do things we know we shouldn't because something tells us we have to."

Eddie felt his feet lifting off the floor. The room began to pound and he was afraid. He couldn't move. Wanda's eyes were looking right through him again like they did during the heat wave last summer.

Eddie looked like he was hypnotized. Wanda's voice was softer and lower, "You're going to need fallible people your whole life, Eddie, because there aren't any other kind... and you are the kind of person who will need to have people. It's hard to explain. In fact it is something you learn that can't be explained... you have to learn it by yourself, with someone else."

The street lamp over the Monroe's front yard popped on, casting a striped shadow from the venetian blinds across the floor, and over Wanda's legs. Eddie stood in the center of the room in the dark looking toward Wanda's shadowy figure in the rocking chair. She finished her coffee. Eddie walked to the screen door.

"Eddie, will you turn on the sprinkler?" The screen door swung open and Eddie walked out. Wanda smiled to herself and made her decision. If the boy left for the game, then fine. If he came back in here, then fine. It was up to him.

The rain-bird began its staccatto blasts. Reversed itself and repeated its blasts. Reversed itself and repeated its blasts, again. Brenda Lee came up on the radio. Eddie walked through the screen door.

"Eddie, have you and Sherry gone all the way?" Her voice had the same quivering sound Eddie's had had earlier. He remembered Wanda's voice saying, fallible.

"No, we haven't."

"Have you ever wanted to?"

"Yes."

"Do you want to?" He watched the rocking chair shift forward and saw Wanda's figure looming in the dark. He was frozen. He felt like he was getting sick. She moved closer toward him, until he could see her face clearly inches away. She looked like she was summoning up courage. The moment it scared Eddie to see her under that kind of strain, her face relaxed into a smile. Her fingers touched Eddie's rigid hands, hanging stiffly at his side. The touch felt like an electrical storm. Her hair brushed the side of his face, her cheek pressed against his jaw. Her voice joined Brenda Lee's "...please accept my a-pol-ogy... I was too young... and I was to blind to see..." The song ended. Wanda's arms were around Eddie's chest, her breasts pressing lightly against his shirt.

The inside of one of her legs bumped the outside of his thigh. She smiled up at him and said, "Thanks for the dance Eddie." Eddie who felt as though he had gotten older and stronger in the past two minutes said, "You're welcome Wanda." She didn't move. Eddie couldn't stop thinking that a woman was holding him, a woman he had always desired and had always thought was above and beyond him. He couldn't understand what was happening, but her dark face and easy smile were guiding him someplace. He fought off thoughts of the boys, and her husband, and tried desperately to find some type of omen, some sense that the time here was right, and the consequences would not destroy him. A hot breeze from the desert rattled the screen door and blew over them. "Santana," thought Eddie.

"I love this time of day, Eddie. Don't you? I've always thought this was the best time of day."

"It is."

"I'm going to kiss you, Eddie. Is that alright?"

"Yes."

Wanda's lips had more weight, more depth, more demand than any lips Eddie had ever felt. Wanda felt Eddie's lips hesitate, and then join hers. She pulled away slowly, and then kissed him again. There was less hesitation this time. They met, and the intensity increased. She pulled slowly away again. In the next instant their lips touched, her tongue ran over his lips, and his mouth parted slightly. Eddie leaned back, a thin silver thread hung suspended between their lips, snapped and slapped wet against Eddie's chin. Wanda's fingers reached up and wiped his lip and chin, whispering "Sometimes it's hard to keep our dignity at times like these." Eddie smiled, "What are we gonna do, Wanda?" "I think we're going to go to bed Eddie." Eddie's heart pounded so hard he thought he'd faint. "What are we gonna do after that?" "I'm going to drive you to the game." "And after that." "You're gonna play football." They smiled in unison. "And after that?" "Nothing, because the first time is just once. This is your first time..." Wanda's words faded as Eddie realized it was his first time, and that he was in the beginning of his first time, and they were not going to stop here, and that soon he would be lying naked in bed with this woman, and he would be inside of her, and all the images he had ever had would become images he would never forget. "...Eddie... it is your first time isn't it?" "Yes." "It should be with someone you care a lot about, and someone who cares a lot about you, someone you trust... the first time is only..." She lifted her face and kissed him again, her mouth warmer and somehow more pliable, as though it were more alive. "...Just once, and that is all. I promise you, once. Once. And we'll never mention it. We'll never let on that it ever happened, not in front of anyone, and not even when we are alone. I promise. Do you promise?" Eddie couldn't believe that it could be happening. A hotter breeze blew in the door spinning the newspaper along the floor, dogs started barking. "It's the only way it could be, Wanda." Wanda breathed the words "That's right" into his face. She took his hand and led him in the dark toward her bedroom.

The phone rang. Wanda reached over the rocking chair, still holding Eddie's hand and picked up the receiver. Eddie knew it was his mother. "Well, hi. Yeah, he's here. Couldn't hook up for a ride. I thought I'd take him." Her voice sounded exactly like it always did, nothing hidden, nothing deceptive, natural, comfortable. Eddie felt her squeeze his hand as she said, "Why don't we pick you up in about an hour?...Yeah, you do? Oh, great, I'd like to take a shower and change and we'll pick you up at quarter to eight. Great. I know Eddie will be glad you're going. You want to speak to him? Alright." Eddie heard the electrical duplication of his mother's voice in the telephone saying, "See ya" as Wanda put the phone on the hook. "Ok, Eddie?" Her eyes looked bright, at their easy-going, good-natured best. Eddie put his hand in her hair and let the black strands untangle slowly as he slid them from her forehead, over her ear, and down the back of her neck. It had been something he had wanted to do every time he saw her loving hands caressing one of the boys. The tender expression her face held as she touched her children was now on her face and he had brought it to her. His whole body responded, his groin pounded and began to ache. The black eyes closed and her body arched like a cat. Eddie shuddered slightly, and Wanda sensing it, opened her eyes. "C'mon Eddie." Her voice had a final tone, a purpose, a warm determination. As they walked by the rocker Eddie put one hand on the chair and pushed it gently. They disappeared into the shadow toward her room. As the rocker tilted back and forth, back and forth, in and out of the striped shadows of the venetian blinds, to the music of the rain bird, the rattling screen door, the hot wind outside and a woman's voice singing on the radio.

A T-SHIRT, PHEROMONES, AND GRIEF

(March 9th, 1958 – San Diego, California)

"Well, it's up to you, always was…" The boy could hear the drawling voice hanging in the air. The big man had been dead now for almost two months. The boy was crying, not from the beating he had just endured as much as from the aching in his chest. The boy felt he could never get the air he needed again, as though he would never breathe free like he could a couple of months ago.

He kept hearing the adage "rug pulled out from under him." He felt ashamed. He hadn't been able to put up more than a half-hearted effort at the defense of the big man's name. He had put on a show of fighting back, but his heart wasn't in it and it made him feel like a liar. The jeering and the laughing and the names he was called were still echoing in his head as he started to cry again. He hid his face in his elbow and watched the spit and tears congeal and drip from his open, sobbing mouth, landing on the gray cement, making patterns as it dropped and shook from his sobbing chest.

"…Always will be," continued the big man's drawl. The boy could see the invisible smile following the remembered words. He cried harder. The sobbing sounded deep and foreign, a shaking, breaking call to a couple of months ago.

Abruptly the boy rose to his feet. With both hands flat against his face, he smeared away the wet and slipped his fingers into his hair, combing the long strands flat. Not crying any longer, but still sobbing because his body couldn't stop, he walked over to the big man's tool box. He pulled it open by the chrome handle and opened it like a tackle box. The big man's wife began playing the piano in the front room. She stopped. The boy started saying to himself, "Don't stop, keep playing... keep playing." There was a pause, and then she started playing again. He closed his eyes, wishing she would play forever. He was relieved that she wouldn't come out and find him with the big man's belongings.

Around the corner of the house and out in the street the boy could hear sounds. The other boys were out there arguing about something. It was the standard declaration of dominance, not a real dispute. There could be no real dispute. There could be no opposition to that voice. It belonged to the ultimate victor. The boy's feelings weren't as hard against the victor as they were against the victor's friends – the boys who would egg the victor on, who would make the victor think, in his stupidity, that his show of force and brutality was admirable, who would use the boy as a sacrifice until the next time the victor felt threatened and would pound, kick, and beat his next victim.

For the past couple of months all of the victor's anger and stupid, huge violence had been directed at the boy. The boy was tired and feeling an essential part of his coming manhood suffering and dying and cringing. He would renew his resolve daily, trying to stand upright against the demoralization of his heart, which had been breaking since the big man died. He quietly moved the tools around in the box, freeing the white T-shirt stuffed into one corner.

He held the T-shirt out at arm's length. It stretched out in front of him and its bottom seam nearly touched the cement. He tried to see the big man inside the flat material. It was useless.

There was a time once when the boy had promised to take care of the big man's dogs. The boy had shown up every day except one, and the big man found out somehow. The boy had taken the long way home from school winding through the canyons avoiding the route the victor and his friends might take. When he got home it was almost dark and his mother wouldn't let him leave the house until morning. When the big man asked the boy about it, the boy lied. "Boy, I'm going to tell you something and you'd better remember it. You'll be better off putting your faith in what you know is on earth, instead of what might be in heaven. You are on your own. Nobody gets to heaven holding hands and no one can help you get there. Most people fail to realize that what goes on up there, is determined by what goes on down here. If you give your word, like you did to me, then you have to do everything you can to keep it. It's hard, and you'll have to face it everyday. The devil always gives you a good reason to do wrong. Keep your word, boy. It's one of the most important things you've got. And if someone loves you, and I love you, then you never have to lie to them. And if someone hates you, then never let them make you make less of yourself."

The big man took several deep breaths, broke into a sweat and then looked at the boy and smiled. "The weight you're willing to put on your shoulders here on earth gives you the strength to climb up to those pearly gates when the time comes." The last thing he told him before he turned and walked into his house was, "Listen to your own voice. Not your fears, or your feelings, good or bad. Listen to what's in your heart and do what it tells you."

The boy never really understood what the big man meant most of the time. The words seemed crazy. It was the big man who made sense, not his words. The big man always seemed to be trying to help him cross a bridge that could never be crossed. The big man always seemed to be answering, in one way or another, almost by riddles, the only question the boy ever wanted answered: How could a skinny, awkward kid ever hope to become a man? "Boy, what are you talking about? Now I have heard everything. How am I gonna become a man? Silliest shit I ever heard. You are a boy, so you are going to become a man. What kind of man? Maybe that's the question. That's a little more important. You're a boy now, so you'll be a man soon enough. You've been given a brain and a body and a heart, right? Well, if you've been given these things then they are yours to use. To use.

Don't worry about having it or not. Hell, you might have been given it by mistake. Just put it to use. Nothing else counts. Not what you or anyone else says, thinks, or even does to you. Now hand me that crescent wrench so I can put it to use and see if I can fix this damn thing before dark."

The boy knew in the world of boys he wasn't much; in the world of men, he appeared to be doomed. Everything the big man did or said seemed to indicate that the boy's opinion of himself was wrong, nearly always summed up with a statement like "Time will tell." It terrified the boy to hear the big man say things like that, or "Don't worry so much. Ya know 99% of the things folks worry about never even happens." It was especially upsetting to hear the big man mention love, as though it was a real thing and would someday play a large part in the boy's life. The boy took the T-shirt and pressed it against his face. He could smell the big man. He didn't notice that the piano had stopped its music, or that the curtains to the big man's back room were being parted by the big man's wife. He didn't see the puzzled look on her face as she watched the boy breathing through the shirt. Her husband of forty years was gone. The boy was trying to contact his departed soul through the shirt. She knew the boy meant no harm, and she understood the indulgence of pain his action represented. She also knew it was wrong, contrary to life; would weaken him. She watched the boy carefully put the shirt back into the tool box, push the box into the patio corner, turn silently and climb over the fence and disappear.

The boy was challenged as soon as he hit the street. He tried to walk past the cat calls and the derisively chucked bottle caps and curses. The ultimate victor began to cross the street, cutting him off. The boy's heart pounded; he tried to walk imperceptibly faster. He heard the words again, "nigger lover." He heard them ten thousand times. The big man's front door was hidden in the shade; the old woman was watching. She saw the boy stop. She saw the victor walk toward him faster and hit him on the ear. She saw the boy's hand go up, and saw him cringe and cower as the next blow landed on his face, the other boys surrounding him in a half circle. She saw the boy respond to a comment from one of the other boys and watched them fall to the ground, twisting and swinging. The fight was brief. She saw the boy standing over the other boy. But the triumph of her husband's defender was shortlived. The victor waited a second and then pounded the boy down next to his opponent, who then took to his feet and began kicking as the victor continued to land thudding punches to the boy's head.

The boy lay on the ground, humiliated and silent. The boys and the victor wandered slowly back to the curb, pausing momentarily for a stray kick, another punch, another spat epithet. The wife of the big man walked out to the back patio and removed the T-shirt from the tool box. She washed it that night, folded it neatly and placed it on the window sill in the back window. A couple of days later the boy crept across the neighbor's yard, climbed the fence, and kneeled over the tool box. The woman walked quietly out of the back door. She looked at the boy. "Eddie, this shirt don't fit you yet, but it must be yours." She handed it to the boy, turned around and walked back into her house.

The first time Eddie saw Jenny was in Mexico, at the beach, at a camping ground just south of Rosarita, in September of 1961. He was going to start off the seventh grade within the next couple of weeks, but until then he was with his family and four other families enjoying the heat, the surf, the nights under the stars.

JENNY

Eddie's mother and father were preoccupied with the card game that was now into it's fifth night. There had been the usual passing out, hysteria, vomiting, and hilarity among the nine players. Tequila was fueling a three night run of luck by a one-legged neighbor wearing a straw hat and a loincloth. The others were amazed and enraged at the drunk's ridiculous streak. Each player came with $200, in one dollar bills, most of it presently under the cushion of the stool the straw hatted man sat on, too crazy with the streak to sleep, and unwilling to slow down the pace. Eddie and his friend Robert wondered how long it was going to be before one of them killed him. It was Mexico after all. The game had started with Eddie's aunt Ellen taking most of the hands. But when her husband went back to San Diego, because he had to work, she was seduced by her friend Lois's brother and she lost her inertia. It had to happen, as far as Eddie could tell. Lois' brother had a legendary cock, Ellen looked good in a bathing suit, real good, and her husband liked Lois's brother a lot anyway, and was careless despite Ellen's wandering eye. Eddie watched her walking bow-legged out to the beach at about dawn the night she gave up her streak, furious as hell about the shitty hands she was getting.

The heat was off the next afternoon and the card game was picking up energy, all players present. The guy with the straw hat was rubbing it in as Eddie watched the Tequila bottle being passed between his uncles, "Gotta stay in the game. That's the secret, Ellen." "Just deal you one-legged idiot." The man laughed and raised the ante as the table groaned and Lois's brother told Ellen to "Shut up." Ellen said "Shut me up." The man with the staw hat said, "Yeah, Bill shut her up." Eddie's mother said "Not this again." Eddie's father said, "I'm out," and headed for his tent. Eddie loved it when they got like that.

Eddie saw three horses coming over a sand dune to the north of the encampment so he started walking in that direction. Robert and two Mexican kids had been riding for a couple of hours, hunting rabbits inland. Eddie heard a shrill whistle and saw Raul lifting a pile of gray things in the air above his head. Eddie began a slow lope as they kicked their heels into the ribs of the exhausted nags. The horses shifted their weight back as the boys slid up their necks. A couple of minutes later Eddie was looking up at the three boys sitting barebacked on their mounts, Robert cradling his .22, Arturo looking bored, and tiny Raul wearing a string of bloody dead rabbits over one shoulder. Robert said he'd help with the horses for a few minutes and then meet Eddie to catch the glass off. Surf tonight was nothing to get excited about. Yesterday was the day. Raul split the rabbits with Eddie, and the horsemen rode back inland. Eddie walked back to the camp.

Two station wagons loaded with surfboards blasted down the dirt road toward the camp from the highway, raising a dust cloud forty feet in the air, skidding, spinning and bouncing along at about 50 miles an hour. The entire camp containing about twenty families started hollering at them. The car continued blasting its way into camp. Eddie stood mid-stride watching the cars and noticing the girls inside.

The station wagons spun to a halt. Doors swung open. Girls jumped out. Doors slammed shut. Brief partings were exchanged, "Later", "See ya." The station wagons blew out the road they entered and five girls walked toward a palm covered pavilion, carrying a cooler, a record player, and a box of 45's. Five angels walked toward the pavilion. Eddie immediately envied the boys driving those station wagons. MSA? Wind and Sea? Didn't matter. The girls knew who they were, knew what they had, and knew what they were doing. A couple of campers came up to register complaints about the dust, the racket and the dangerous driving, pointing to little kids playing 200 yards distant. The girls walked along until one of them said, "Yeah, we know. They always drive like that." In the distance the station wagons headed south on the regular roadway at a controlled speed. The girls walked under the rustling palm leaves, sat against the support pillars and fell immediately to sleep. Eddie lingered around the card game with his eye on the pavilion. Bill asked him why he didn't go over and say hi. Eddie said he had to get the rabbits ready for dinner. "Why? Robert shot 'em, let him skin 'em." Eddie shrugged, "I bet they'd get three at the most." Ellen staring at her cards shot a look at Eddie's mother. "Runs in the family, I guess." Eddie's mother made a sniggering sound and muttered, "Stupid bet, place is hopping with bunnies." Eddie picked up the rabbits, walked over to the side of one camper and said, "He only had six shots." Bill said, "Well, go on over there and get something bloody." Eddie's mother settled further in her chair. Ellen said, "Oh, Bill... you nasty man." The man with the straw hat drawled "The only blood anybody'll get from bunnies around here are from the kind with long ears," and shot a glance at the pavilion. Eddie tore the skin down the rabbits backs, cut their guts out, their heads off, and tried to ignore the sound of his father puking behind the tent. The card game mumbled on.

With his ankles in the cool water and his hands leaving a bloody trail in the foam Eddie could just see the top of the palm fronds from the pavillion. Robert walked up carrying one fin. "Fuck, man. Did you see the girls at the pavilion?" "Nope." "Unbeleeevvable." "Some surfers dropped them off about twenty minutes ago." "Bullshit." "Let's check it out." "Ok, let's cool off first." The whining sound of a spinning reel sang behind them as a line with a lead sinker and three hooks baited with mussels flew above them and out beyond the surf line. The boys began running into the surf slowly, hurdling each shelf of white water, until waist deep they submerged. In an instant they pulled the fins over a foot, and like otters stroked out into the surf. The waves to the outside were pretty good size and of perfect shape. Robert got most of the rides. Eddie was preoccuppied with the girls in the pavilion. As each swell rose, he'd turn, hoping not to see station wagons. "Robert, c'mon… let's go in."

A minute later they were banging the water out of their ears and heading toward the card game. They heard yelling coming from the table. Wordlessly they turned at an angle that led directly toward the silent pavilion. Eddie, looking at his brown feet, mumbled, "Fuck that shit." "Eddie…", the sound in Robert's voice said, " Look at that." Eddie looked up and saw an angel in a pair of Levis walking in the shade carrying a record player. The boys walked to a broken-down rusted truck hulk sitting to one side of a cement slab which began sending music over the campsite. The boys climbed in the rusted cabin, Robert got his cigarettes from under the dashboard and lit up. The boys watched the girls dancing together between their propped-up feet on the rusted dash. Robert and Eddie sat in silence, occasionally double-taking each other as one or the other girls moved in perfect, casual, almost bored, timing. Robert exhaled a cloud saying, "Oh, my God." Eddie shook his head.

The girls had already attracted plenty of attention on their arrival, but since the main water source for the camp was a spigot on one side of the pavilion, the campers had plenty of reason to nose around. Their dancing had drawn a crowd. The elderly couple that Eddie and Robert liked were the first ones there. They had immediately found it possible to talk to the girls, and the old man was given a beer from the cooler. The old man said something that made one of the girls laugh when she extended the beer. As her body language responded to the laugh, she pulled the little old man under her arm, hugged him, and beamed the most beautiful smile the boys had ever seen. "Oh, my God. She's…"

words failed Robert. The stack of records dropped one by one, and one or another of the girls would dance easily and casually, while one of them leafed through a magazine. Eddie was watching her. She had long straight waist-length hair that gave credence to the term, flaxen. The eyes following the pages were blue. She had a cleft lip which, it immediately seemed, held absolutely no consequence to her. She sat with her knees hugged up against her chest, her jeans straining with its contents – a perfect butt. She and her friends were of that infuriating age just beyond the range of Eddie and Robert. They must have been 14 or 15 to the boys 12. The youngest kids in the campground had joined the oldest, and the most beautiful. Two of the girls were dancing with kids about 6 years old. Another record dropped, a song Eddie had never heard before. The song was from a girl group and began with a chorus, "Wah, whaa, wah, oooh, wah, tusi..." The five girls began to dance in earnest with each other, the little kids pairing off in participation on the periphery. Eddie and Robert may have breathed three times each in the next three minutes. Their eyes may have only jutted half an inch out of their sockets. Their jaws bounced on their gulping Adams apples. Eddie watched the girl put the magazine aside and slowly shuffle across the smooth cement floor, singing with the record. The girls sounded as though they had made the record, adding to the sound in perfect harmony, and raising their voices higher as they realized the covered cement floor gave them a reverberating amplification.

A little boy was raised above the head of Eddie's favorite, and spun in a slow circle looking down at the girl's smiling face, her lip pulling her mouth slightly off to one side, and her eyes bringing a contagious grin on the little boy's face, who was already plainly, and totally, in love. Eddie envied the boy in the air, and felt almost ashamed at the envy. He felt uncomfortable identifying with the little boy, who was getting the ride of a lifetime, but couldn't help himself. The song ended. The girl ran over to the record player and put the needle back on the record and clicked the switch. By this time Eddie and Robert had climbed out of the truck like zombies and walked mesmerized to the side of the elderly couple. The little bald man tilting back the beer, gave Eddie a wink. His wife, clasped Robert's arm in her skinny blue-veined hands and said, "Oh, dear. Aren't they wonderful?" Robert managed to say, "Yeah." The music carried the girls to within a few feet of the two motionless adolescents, and the elderly couple. The blond girl had her back to Eddie and he watched the end of her pony tail flick in time with the bass. The old man cleared his throat just as the blond girl turned to smile in his direction. The old man's voice at Eddie's left said, "Do you want to dance?" Eddie felt the old man's shaky hands push him onto the cement in front of the girl. Eddie stood frozen. The man's wife laughed. The girl closed the distance between Eddie and herself, and took his hands in hers. Eddie was gone, absolutely and entirely in sync with the girl. If he had had the slightest chance to think, had not been entirely mesmerized he undoubtedly would have stiffened to a board and died of embarrassment. There was no reason for him to be able to move with her, there was no reason for him to adopt the male version of her female interpre-tation. There was no precedent in his life for catching rhythm with his body, and there was no evidence to anybody watching that he hadn't done this a thousand times. Only the blond girl knew, and maybe the little boy who earlier had had a similar feeling as he spun above this angel's head, riding on her out-stretched arms, safe in the air. The music stopped. One of the girls pulled the plug on the record player, the records were gathered, put in the box. Another beer was tossed to the elderly man, who snatched it one-handed out of the air. The station wagons appeared from out of nowhere. A tall boy of about 16, and another boy of just a couple of precious years more than Eddie was by his side. The younger boy called out "Jenny...", and the blond girl ran over to him and was spun once in his arms. She climbed up his broad brown arms and whispered something into his ear. The girl ran out to the station wagon. The boy grabbed the cooler and they disappeared into the backseat. They spun around in a dust cloud and the girl's long arm extended out of the window and waved goodbye to the elderly couple. The boy beside her grinned out of the window and revealed two tin front teeth. The instant they saw that shining silver smile Robert and Eddie said at the same time, "Jimmy Blackwell." That said it all, the coolest and most famous surfer in San Diego. The station wagon blasted down the road, turned on its lights and the red dots disappeared down the dusty road. As Eddie began to walk back to the card game, he noticed the little boy looking at him. Eddie winked at him, saying "Fun, huh?" Robert mumbled, "Shit, Eddie, Fred- A- fucking- Staire." "Yeah, twinkle toes," sighed Eddie. As they watched the white headlights turn south on the main road leading deeper into Mexico, they realized they'd have a lot to think about that night.

Here He Comes...

It turned out there were a lot of nights to think about Jenny, because in the next five years her path and Eddie's crossed frequently. When Eddie hit the huge boom-town Junior High School that fall, he saw her walking past his wood shop class on her way home with a girlfriend. Ninth graders free by the sixth period, seventh graders with two more to go. He stared out the window watching the girls shifting their notebooks and laughing. The shop teacher growled "Burnett," and Eddie returned to his scale drawing of the wagon wheel lamp they would be making that semester. A few seconds later the teacher barked "Buurnnett!" Eddie looked up to see the class of boys smiling at him and turned red realizing he must have been singing "Cathy's Clown" a little too loudly under his breath.

Swish!

In the early spring Eddie and Robert had gone to watch the league high school basketball championships and watched Jimmy sink 42 points, most of them rafter-high bombs from the outside, as the gymnasium went nuts. Eddie asked around about Jenny and was told she was down at a communal beach house keeping company with a blues quartet that was playing later that night downtown. When the final buzzer sounded as his winning shot exploded the net, Jimmy blasted out of the gym exit for parts unknown, to the astonishing spectators. Next Monday at school Robert's older sister told them that Jimmy had sat-in with the quartet playing sax until 3 in the morning. Furthermore, and to his credit, Jimmy was going to be kicked out of school again and off the team forever because he ditched school to go up to L.A. and sit in on a recording session! Robert's sister walked across the street to the high school and Robert and Eddie stood there awestruck, contemplating the cool lives of Jenny and Jimmy.

Dying Swan

Eddie was completing a crucifix swan dive, propelled with a force sounding like a choral roar sliding down a glassy wall, heading for the welcome imprisonment of a closed out 8' wave next to Crystal Pier. The object was to be overwhelmed. He was seeking, day in and day out, the awe that catches the breath, before the lungs fill with dread and delight, under the surface on the edge of the Pacific Rim, cooperating zen-style, spun and twisted, trying to maintain a tight fetal grip, while the washing machine tried to pull him apart. He shuddered at his own ecstatic smile as he ran out of air and his vision turned a dark reddish blue. It seemed the cleanest, most honorable, and most satisfying way to go.

Back in elementary school he had experienced a sensation that was akin to drowning, but it lacked the physical release that permitted him to use the experience as a message, a symbol. Instead of screaming inside his head the demand to survive, it felt as though his soul had imploded on it's host. He noticed the deformed hand of his third grade teacher. As a third grader does, he registered the desolate-hopeless pain the image transferred, with complete empathy and surprise.

It explained why Jenny was so cool. Jenny lying in the sand talking with her girlfriends about cultural topics beyond Eddie's scope. Books, movies, themes to songs, make-up, fashion, cars, and older brothers. Eddie was dumbstruck recognizing the power of compensation. How what might seem tragic on sight, might essentially be an asset, even an advantage. Maybe the friendship between Eddie and Jenny was based on something they had in common, some genetic error or difference that was revealed as a scar on Jenny's face, but was hidden somewhere inside Eddie's thoughts or spirit. Dragging himself out of the surf, exhausted and spent, the tips of his fins slapping in the water beneath him he thought of Jenny's scarred lip, and his own incapacity to communicate the things he saw and felt.

Jenny was exactly what she was, and it was enough for anyone, even Jenny. Eddie was not anything near to what he was, and it was lacking for everyone, especially Eddie. The sentence ran through his head, "Who's scarred?" Jenny had composure, self-assurance, adamant self-possession enough to lend it to anyone seeming to need it. She got it from a scarred lip, and the courage to face it. Eddie wished he could identify his internal scars, in order to try to find the courage to face them. As Eddie walked into the hot sand toward the towel Jenny was lying on he felt as though he were walking into a sort of church. She was annointed by direct knowledge, knowledge from birth, knowledge she could not escape, and reminded by the second, that life is not fair. She would have to seduce life and she did. She held up her end of the bargain. She filled those hours making friends laugh with her re-grounding gentle humor, making wisecracks that carried the long shot into a pin-point deflating bullseye. She had never in the years they had been friends once stooped to an instant of cruelty. It amazed Eddie. He watched her from a distance and continually fell under her spell. It was as though her words and face attracted him to follow her to a place where the fears weren't imagined, where pain wasn't temporary, to the place where she lived. As he neared the place where Jenny and her friends gathered in the sun, he thought back to that moment in the third grade when he stood transfixed, looking at his teacher's terrified eyes.

He saw the hem of her skirt flicking down the hall, he heard the clickety pattern of her heels reminding him of the weird beat of the wild hen faking an injured retreat leading the predator away from her hidden nestlings. She was carrying her deformed hand inside of her purse, a place that could and did, for the first time, draw Eddie's attention to it. In the classroom she must have felt safe, and therefore the kids felt safe as well, seeing her hand but not registering its difference, or seeing it as a source of shame and pain. Out here she clutched the purse in a give-away that was desperate. Eddie wanted to cry as he saw his teacher turning her back on her own beauty, hiding the portion of herself that made her whole. She was so beautiful, carrying proportions of a movie star with innocence and a complete lack of vanity. Permitting an eight-year-old's face to be buried in her Vargas bosom. Her tiny waist encircled in little-girl-pal-arms. Her smile was devastating, inspiring the children to please her. But at that moment in the hall, traveling from this place to that, surrounded by strangers and out in the open, her shoes clicked too fast and her blond head snapped from side to side, tilted with a studied staunch challenge, her eyes insane and terrified, a tortured smirk taking the place of her smile. Eddie remembered the horror pogoing on his guts and bouncing off the base of his brain making him lightheaded and nauseous as he absorbed his teacher's mysterious nightmare.

SLOW DANCING IN '66

The end of the summer brought the next football season. Eddie was walking into an after-game dance nodding thanks to the kids whispering "Nice game," as he moved into the hall looking for Jenny. Junior Osuna walked up and indicated the spot where Jenny was dancing. Eddie wasn't sure if he should go to her immediately or wait a few more minutes. He had a feeling that compelled him to her. Junior nudged him with his elbow. As Eddie looked down at Junior's profile, which was locked in the direction of Jenny, he took the proffered half-pint of Bacardi. He elbowed the boy next to him and the Bacardi passed along the line of boys leaning against the wall in the dark, listening to San Diego's reigning band Sandy and the Classics playing "Hitch-hike".

Jenny was dressed in black, with her hair shining in the red and blue lights' cast from the makeshift stage. She had lost weight in the last week. Never having been anything but thin before, her too skinny arms swung in time with the music. She had a peculiar luminous glow, like a ghost. Her cheeks were sunken and her eyes dark holes in a stoic face. Her head was tilted down and her hair was falling forward from her jaw line helping to hide any expression. Jenny was doing what she always had done every dance Eddie could remember. She was dancing in her inimitable style, and just a little bit better than any kid in the place. But tonight she was dancing alone. The hair on Eddie's neck stood on end.

Jenny could lift the whole room to a sway, and a stop, a turn and a drop, an increase, and a decrease of energy all this absolutely on time, until every kid in the place was secure and euphoric, giving each other accepted half smiles and furtive glances as they followed her trail along the coolest interpretation of those too cool rhythm and blues.

Tonight Jenny had it all to herself, no one followed her. She tracked the territory of the beat, and the meaning of the beat and rode the bass all by herself. Any distance along her trail was too close for comfort for anyone dancing with her, except when every fifth or sixth song became a slow ballad. As the first slow notes began, and the elbows in the dark hall lifted under the lights and settled around the necks of each pair of dancers, a different boy would weave his way to Jenny to take his turn in her arms. Eddie observed one of Jimmy's closest friends lose it completly when Jenny managed to give him a kiss and one of the smiles that reminded him of a time that wasn't going to come back. The boy left in a bee line for the side exit with the sound of the push-handle door slamming into the wall outside in the night, while the Classics finished the last chorus of "You'll Lose a Good Thing."

The parents who had volunteered as chaperones for this after-game dance noticed the pall over the floor. There was no laughing, no loud talking or horseplay in the entire gym. The usual three or four hundred kids were packed on the floor and the shoulders and hips dipped and waved in unison song after song, but other than the music, and the low murmur of voices, the place was silent and dark. There had always been tearful exits at these dances, the result of unrequited love, or discovered betrayal of the early teen variety, but tonight struck the five or six parents as something different. They patrolled the perimeters of the hall, and spoke quietly to each other in small huddles, sensing something happening but not knowing what it was. A couple of parents made an effort to ask a few kids but none of them, from the most mature and cooperative to the most anxious to please sophomore would give an answer. The parents noticed a distinct coldness from each kid, as the question was posed.

Jenny was followed into the bathroom by four or five friends. The gymnasium seemed to swell in a sigh of collected relief. The room returned to something more normal for a dance during the next few songs, and the voices got a little louder.

Eddie looked at the other boy standing across the girls' bathroom door. "Eddie, ya wanna go next?"

Eddie answered with a nod of his head and the older boy walked over to the open spot next to Junior Osuna. Eddie could hear the girls walking toward the door as the sax began its climb up Harlem Nocturne. Jenny balked at the entrance to the huge cavern, and then seeing Eddie walked quickly toward him. Her face pressed against his neck and her hips drove into him. Her body trembled furiously beneath her black dress. They began their slow dance.

As they held each other tighter she transfered her rage and pain to Eddie until it was trembling into his bones. As Jenny whispered one word into Eddie's ear, instinct told them both that it was a waste, it was wrong, and it was a crime against nature that Jimmy, or anyone had to die in this new war in Vietnam. The inexplicable wisdom of their youth predicted that many more deaths would soon follow Jimmy's. Jenny whispered, "Promise?" And knowing what Jenny was asking Eddie replied, "Yes, I promise."

HAPPY BIRTHDAY

1967. The accelerator pedal was on the floor. Robert Monroe and his younger brother Grant are heading to T.J., Sin City, Aunt Jane, Tijuana. Just a twenty minute car-flight down Interstate 5. Their mother Wanda has finally succumbed to permanent depression and never leaves her rocking chair. Their older sister from Texas is married, unhappily, with her third kid on the way. Eddie Burnett is driving. Tonight's excursion "South" is to finish off Grant's eighteenth birthday. The Vietnam war is central in these boys' lives. The war has polarized the society in which they live. Lots of rhetoric is tossed around, but the boys know the bottom line, and it's profit over blood, their blood, Vietnamese blood. The practice is now common to cross the border in the trunks of cars driven by an eighteen-year-old friend for a night of drinking, whoring, and increasingly confronting Marines from Camp Pendleton 60 miles to the north. Tijuana is no-man's land, patrolled by brown uniformed Federales who throw servicemen and rowdy Americans into the mad-house that serves as a jail. The boys and Marines are found in "off-limit bars", the Federales serve as a natural buffer between them.

Eddie Burnett has changed since you saw him last, constantly furious behind a cold-as-stone facade. His wide-eyed innocent perspective has become a dangerous angry rebellion. He is driving his boyhood friends to the notorious Green Note bar brothel, a few blocks north of Avenida Revolución. Robert is certifiable, hopped up on huge quantities of speed, tequila, and anything else he can get his hands on. He has "checked out" for hours, now lucid and inspired, and then for days, vicious, irrational, and incredibly paranoid. Grant has been trying in recent months to be a stabilzing force between the outright hostility of Robert, and the repressed anger and sadness of Eddie. In recent months they have been wrecking cars at an astonishing rate. They know where they are heading. It's 1:45 a.m. and they are passing through San Ysidro.

Cars are honking and brakes are screeching. Eddie is tailgating a Cadillac, then passing it and slamming on his brakes. He sees an "America Love it or Leave It" decal in the rear window. "Caaadddaaaalaaack..Caddaaaalack" repeats Eddie. The window on the passenger side goes down and Robert leans out beyond his hips with Grant grabbing the waist band of his Levis. "Fuck you... Yeah you... Love to, you blue haired old bitch..." Eddie sputters "Fucking little flag waving in the plastic decal." Eddie jerks the car in front of the enraged Caddy and slams on the brakes again. The car lurches to one side and flies along the cyclone fence for a couple of hundred yards and pulls to a stop. Robert looking in the side rear view mirror comments disapprovingly, "Ah, Eddie that wasn't even close." Eddie entirely calm and looking for another song on the radio besides "Light My Fire" which he hates, comments off-handedly, "Well, it's the thought that counts."

Robert climbs over the seat and pulls Grant into a head lock singing, "Happy birthday to you, happy birthday to yoooooo, happy birthday dear Graaaaannnnnttaaaa, happppy birthdayyy tooooo yoooo. Eighteen! My little brother eighteen. Man-oh-man. You are now killin' age little brother, old enough to bleed, old enough to butcher." Robert begins turning his pockets inside out, then he raises a finger in comic recognition, and pulls off his pants. From the front seat, "Robert, what the fuck are ya doin'?" "What am I doin'?, what am I doin'? I am getting high on my brother's killin' age birthday. I happen to have a stash of little bennies up my ass and I think we should indulge before we hit the border." Grant trying to calm Robert down informs him that he is a little too high already. "No such thing. Never happen. That is to say it is all relative, little relative. Uh sorry, that was bad. But inside this tin foil package that has remained stuffed under my young warm balls are at least 15 little white pills." Eddie tries to get the word to Grant to get the pills out of Robert's hands. "Grant..." Robert starts laughing, "Oh yeah, Grant, what are you gonna do? Hey, do you think Indians got high? They did. They were the stoniest motherfuckers in the world." Grant trying to slow Robert down a little. "Those Indians are dead, Robert." "That is what the white man wants you to think, they're still around – someplace." Robert opens his mouth over the mound of pills in his palm. Grant pulls on his arm and Robert jerks violently away. "Hey!! Now relax. There are up to twenty little whites melting in my hand presently. I will take them all immediately, or I will split them with my best friend Eddie. How's that? I am willing to share. Hey. Where the fuck is the fucking brew? Who took the brew?" Grant cracks three beer cans open in rapid succession. Robert downing one and reaching for another, "Ahhh yesss. Now then. We drink the brew as befits a wake, which is your birthday, brother, in a manner of speaking, and Eddie, you and I split these bennies." Robert climbs back into the front seat. "Open the old mouth Eddie. Stick out the old tongue." Eddie opens his mouth, and sticks out his tongue. "Good. Now then. One for you, one for me, one for you, one for me." This procedure continues with Eddie laughing as the whites pile onto his tongue, and Robert chews his. "Watch the fucking road there, Burnett. Ok, one for you, one for me... Fuck! Dropped one. Hold it a second. Ah, here it is, one more for me." They start laughing. Eddie swallows his tongue full, washing it down with a hit of beer, checking the rearview mirror. Robert finishes the rest. Grant mumbles from the rear window, his elbow hanging out in the wind, his head resting on his shoulder and the air blasting in his face, "Happy now?" "Yeah, for the time being," responds Robert in an entirely different and devastated tone. Silence in the car for several minutes. Robert looks out at the landmark electrical plant near the highway and mutters, "Crazy Horse. What a great fuckin' name."

BOY IN THE AIR 3

He was walking past a church which stood on a corner, painted brown and doing nothing and nobody any good. He resented that church, felt at odds with it, because he had been in head-long pursuit of forbidden kicks, and flirting with foreboding consequences. Strolling along the streets surrounding his campus, full of the rewards of athletic life, strong as a cat, fast as anything, daring, mean and violent. He was getting stoned as he walked along with his buddy, who he didn't know at the time was into rape. They were passing a fat joint between them as night was falling. The last light of the sun had left the spring air warm and intoxicating. His buddy had an evil atmosphere that made Eddie feel secure, because he sensed that he had the worst case scenario walking right beside him, so there was nothing to imagine that could be worse. Eddie had begun running dope across the border and part of his reward for those nocturnal labors was an endless supply of drugs. So, Eddie was walking along, keeping his secret, and his buddy keeping his, when he said to Eddie, "Uh, there's a cop behind us."

In 1969 in San Diego you were on your way to jail for a joint. Eddie had just been busted again, and was out on a hard-to-get-in-this-case Own Recognizance. Some local sports fanatic had come to his aid, willing to pay any weird price to tell his friends he was "helping" the star. Eddie was very glad to be out. He hated jail. He turned slowly, as he swallowed the joint, and adjusted the baggie under his nuts, expecting to see the much feared cruiser down the block. To his dismay the car was right beside him. Two cops looking out of the window, one saying, "Hey, get in the car. I want to talk to you."

Eddie stood there with his hair down to his shoulders in sunburnt coils they call "dreads" today, shirtless, with those late teenage constantly-worked out muscles slapped on his bones, baggy defiant Levis under the heels of his Adidas. Eyes blood red, angry mouth snarling "What did you say?" The delivery dripping with the disrespectful inflection that ends the sentence with an unspoken meaning that says, "Fool." The car stopped and the cop began to move his arm on the door to get out. Eddie leaned off the curb and pressed his weight against the car door. His buddy was frozen in his tracks. Eddie put his face close to the face of the cop, who for a second was taken by surprise and had failed to grab a handful of Eddie's hair. Eddie repeated in increasing volume word by word, "I-ain't-getting-in-no-fucking-car."

Eddie took off straight down the road. It surprised him when the cop who drove nearly had the tires lit in reverse by the time Eddie had cleared the rear bumper by twenty yards. The car beside him was rocking wildly to the left and right screeching black smoke.

Across an intersection another cop car was making a two-wheel turn through a red light. Another one peeled out from behind the church. Set up. For what? Eddie realized they had been surrounded and his determination to escape doubled. He ran out into the middle of the street and drew two cars toward him, then reversed and blasted across the church parking lot. The car from the intersection approached siren blasting, lights spinning, gaining speed to head him off.

The only thing at the end of the parking lot was a cliff that dropped into a deep brush canyon. The car was heading straight at him, the intersection point would be the edge of the cliff. The cops hit the brakes, the screeching stretched for ten seconds of sliding burning rubber. The car was just barely under control and Eddie's legs were spinning in the headlights. He saw the black canyon looming beneath him. Step by step he approached the lip of the rim without the slightest drop in speed. The car spun in a circle of smoke and dirt. Eddie planted his left foot on the edge of the cliff, and jumped up and out, full speed above the canyon. Eddie hung briefly in the suddenly silent night air. He felt the cops' frustration and awe behind him, knowing they were hoping like hell he'd break his 60-foot drop on a concrete corner, or a pile of cement blocks, or with a trimmed branch between his legs. As Eddie began to drop he repeated to himself, "If I can move, I can get away."

As he gained speed he began to expect some awful conclusion to this flight. It was plain that the cops were going to have to conclude that Eddie was willing to go to any length to avoid their smug arrest, the humiliating ride downtown, to say nothing of their resisting arrest excuse to beat him without regret or explanation. He began falling faster, the speed of the run and the blast of the takeoff overcome by an increasing speed in the dark, just as dark brush appeared under him, Wham. A leg-collapsing, back-jarring, teeth-gnashing, neck-snapping, impact. Eddie immediately relaxed and began assessing the damage. Ankles intact, back unbroken, eyes unpoked, wrists and elbows skinless but functional. He was on his feet crashing a trail down into the depths of the canyon floor. Flashlights pointed beams from the cliff edge, searching in vain. Eddie heard the cops mumbling, and saw more headlights converge on the rim. Twenty-five minutes later he was in his room at the beach. They caught his buddy though, got him identified and convicted on four counts of rape and aggravated assault. Gave him three years. Eddie never saw him again.

WINGED SHOES AND A SHIELD

Inside the camper, the street light lends a silver glow to the reeking blue waves of marijuana hanging over the bunk. The ice pick rattles the silverware drawer in response to the figure jerking under the blanket. The rhythm accelerates into a brief moment of frenzy and the figure unfolds, rising to his knees before the window. He freezes a second and then punches the curtain with four jolts of semen, adding to the wet weight hanging on the thin white cotton. The voice, caught in the strain of the effort, sputters, "Four."

Eddie squints at his watch which reads 2:30 a.m. Still coming on. Perfect. He takes another tab. He wipes the sweat from the back of his neck, feeling an increase in fear and anger as he calculates the three and a half hours that remain until dawn. He examines the curtain as he wonders if, at this pace, he will splatter that curtain two or three more times before the cock crows, so to speak.

If these past sixty seconds were a video installation in some chic art spot, the viewer would see that a classic warrior-boy-statue – Perseus standing on a corpse holding a woman's severed head at arm's length, has somehow come to life, revived and cleaned of the dust of centuries and – drenched in sweat induced by alcohol, speed, hysteria and acid – has made the long journey to jack off in a camper parked around the corner from the U.S. Armed Forces Induction Center on Wilshire Boulevard in 1971.

The boy stands barefooted in the camper, buttoning his Levis with one hand over his exhausted dick and cracking another Colt .45 open with the other. Finished with the buttons and half the Colt, he wets his five fingers with the sweat of his forehead, places the tips into a pile of "white crosses," raises the hand with a pill or two stuck to the end of each finger, and inserts each into his mouth. He takes a mouthful of Colt and waits, letting the chalky pills foam into a acrid-tasting mess that seems to bring an electric charge to his mouth's dental work. He swallows. He flicks a match beneath the joint pressed between his lips and the burst of flame reveals the insane red eyes of Eddie Burnett. Insane is the right word—self induced, circumstantial, or a product of amplified empathy. The boy is out of his mind. His eyes change from a bulging hysterical stare into snake-slits of thought. True sailing is dead.

The gods have snuck into hell for awhile to lie in the arms of senseless blood lust, groaning and writhing in a top-and-bottom scene that is beyond comprehension. And let's leave it that way, huh? Besides, as far as Eddie can tell, they're having a real good time.

Eddie feels his muscles swell from his chest up, his heart suddenly pounding in what seems like an empty cavity. Whoa – beginning to rush pretty heavy, Eddie. So he does what he always does when he rushes. He uses the opportunity to knock out another fifty or sixty pushups. Might as well stay in training.

2:32. Eddie thinks he hears the groaning of the souls in flames in Vietnam. He knows outraged spirits are still breathing and are contorted in isolation, sucking in any possible air that does not carry the stench of napalm and My Lai.

The tiny camper fills with shields and appendages laced in leather. Bodies press around him and what has been the silver light of the street lamp becomes a roaring din of carnage. Metal clangs against metal and rings as the echo fills with the grunts of the exertion from hundreds of men dying together in a grisly human ball of horror. Men anchored together in a chain of desperate terror are thrown down, link by link, into an inescapable pit.

Eddie looks to his left and sees a small man, thick-set and whimpering, with snot and tears dripping from his face. The man in front of him shifts his weight constantly, revealing the end of the line – the place that shakes and convulses in an orgy of hand-to-hand death. The man on his right rises on his toes in an effort to see into the coming hell. Catching a glimpse, he screams in rage and despair. The men behind Eddie press their weight, constantly inching him forward.

Eddie thinks about the oncoming hell and the irony that he is moving toward it. Eddie's arms hold a small shield and a short, thick, blunt sword. His vision is obstructed by a nose piece that runs off the front of his helmet. His shins are covered in pounded metal. His mouth is wide open and he is screaming, as he realizes he is less than eight men deep from the front of the stage, where the concentrated effort is a tangled climax of souls departing this bloody earth. He looks to the left side of the swinging, moving mass and sees a blade rise and fall, rise and fall with flesh and blood splattering and spraying in its path. A single man is going berserk, killing one man after another as though they are under a spell and are commanded to cooperate.

Eddie knows in a single flash what he has to do. He locks eyes on the monster who shows no sign of slowing down as he continues to mow down the men before him. Eddie's only chance is somehow to kill that man, who has, at that instant, with a single cracking stroke, lifted the cranium of a man and sent it flying into the ranks beside him. Eddie looks for signs of fatigue in the warrior and the signs are there at last. He watches the arms dropping and the chest heaving. Eddie's hope to live hinges on reaching the man before he can pull back behind the line and recover.

Two men before Eddie fall suddenly. The first is knocked off his feet in surprise with the sweep of one of the man's legs, which catches him under the ankle and spins him onto the ground where his spine is severed with a deft chop behind the neck. The second cannot withstand the press of his shield and slides sideways, exposing his ribs, which are cleaved from bottom to top in a single two-handed stroke.

The warrior slips in the mud and guts at his feet, nearly recovers, then lands heavily pinning his own sword in the mud beneath him. Eddie realizes that the warrior will die at Eddie's

own hands, and not by his planning or his skill, but because of —
what? Fate? Luck?

The men beside Eddie charge into the silver light of the
street lamp after the retreating tangle of hysteria and disappear.
Eddie looks at the camper floor and sees blood running in a stream
under the door and out into the street. He opens his eyes. Medusa.
Perseus holding Medusa's severed head. Eddie parts the curtains
of the window and strikes a match. He looks at his reflection, he
sees the source of his self hatred. Something female inside of him,
distorted and repressed for centuries because of his shame of it.
Hated since the instant he saw the light of day. Over the years the
undeniable female self — the half he felt he had to hide — has been
transformed into his own enemy within, and is becoming the
enemy to all those without. His life and this world was a battle
field. Aries has nothing to do with it. It is Medusa, living right
under the surface, once innocent and beautiful, but warped into
a force that knows nothing but hatred. Eddie stares, as he has stared
countless times searching for her. He brings her into focus and
stares motionless as though he had been turned to stone. Looking
right into his own eyes, his long hair hanging in coils to his
shoulders, twisted into tangles falling over his face like snakes.

Eddie cracks another Colt, inhales a burning cloud into his
raw lungs, holds his breath and thinks: Something has got to be
done about her. Eddie lies back on the bunk, blowing another
cloud to the ceiling, thinking, "Good thing I'm a Gemini, and a
good thing I know Athena. That's all I have to tell them." Eddie
laughs out loud at that one, and washes down a few more whites
with another can of Colt.

Seven hours later he is ushered out of the induction center,
excused by the psychologist on the grounds that he is too insane
for the U.S. Army.

1972

No words came out of his mouth. She thought it was much better that way. He'd knock on her door, or maybe just say her name in the telephone. She knew what he meant. He'd show up in the next five minutes, the next few hours, the next week. "Save me for a second baby. Put me in the shower. Feed me. Get me out of this." She was good to Eddie, always fed him first.

Running in every sense of the word. Magnified gray crystals shining in the beach-fog headlight reflection. Sticky salt air streets sliding his bald tires. Eddie hasn't blinked once in forty minutes. A fragrant pound is under the seat, who knows what is in the trunk. The speed limits are only suggestions that go unheeded. He pulls up on her lawn. Her clothes cling perfectly, she wears only vintage cotton dresses, forties style. She whispers when she talks at all. Her bare feet even whisper on the kitchen floor. She's a tactile girl. She always fed him first.

Five hours later. Fucked. Fucked. Fucked. He's so fucking fucked. What a fucker. He makes Eddie weigh every fucking brick, while he drives too slowly around the same streets of Tecate. It is taking an extra hour. They'll get noticed. Eddie starts reporting lies to him. He knows. Makes him weigh every brick again. Fucker.

Red light. Pulled over. Knew it. Eddie doesn't hear voices. Not Spanish, nothing. This is taking too long. What the hell is going on? He has seen the same Federale pass the front window three times already. What is he waiting for? Hey, maybe he's alone. "Shut up." "You, shut up." The driver sits there in the front seat, both hands visible on the wheel. The great brown makes another slow pass by the windshield. He's checking his notepad. Why isn't he pulling his gun and getting them out of the truck and laying them on the ground beside the road? Will he look back here? Of course he will. Eddie hears the door knob rattle.

The fucker in front is frozen in fear, he is out of plans. He's not calm and sitting there, he's frozen. Eddie hears an echo in his head turning into desperate action, "I am not spending twelve YEARS in a Mexican PRISON." Fuck this. He opens the silverware drawer and pulls out an icepick. The door opens. The Federale's hat pokes in the door, followed by a flashlight. The weight of the camper tilts as the Federale steps in. Eddie grabs him by the skin of his neck. The grime squeezes under his finger nails. The icepick is punched through the back of the brown shirted shoulder. The Federale thrashes with surprising power. Eddie has expected it, and hangs on tighter getting a handful of hair and skin. The icepick slams into the shoulder again, and then again. The Federale is confused, fumbling for his gun. Eddie is furious, "Stupid motherfucker. You should have thought of that before you came in here." Eddie has him on the floor, with one knee pinned on the pistol in the holster, one hand gripping his hair and smashing his face into the linoleum floor. Eddie thinks his knuckles will pop out of their sockets. The man is struggling for his life. Eddie wishes he could convey to him that he is not trying to kill him. But that is impossible. He is screaming. Eddie is screaming. The fucker in the front seat is screaming. Eddie has done it this time. It's a runaway. Make or break. Eddie feels vindicated in the fact that at least he is doing something. He's not sitting up there in the front seat with his carefully weighed twelve year sentences scattered all over the camper. The engine starts up. In seconds they are rolling. The camper door swinging crazily, banging the man's kicking legs. They are picking up night-time-Mexican-smuggler speed. More speed. "He's gotta go."

Eddie begins to change his position. The Federale gets the idea and grips the side of the cabinet. He makes a move for the gun. This leaves one hand with which to grip the cabinet and his legs are bouncing further out of the camper door. Eddie kicks him behind the ear. The Federale's body sags as he makes the decision to hit the asphalt rather than endure another kick. "Lo siento, Adi-fucking-os," and the man slides out the door into the dark. "Fuck you." "What do you mean? What the fuck could I do? You want to go to prison?" "Not for murder." "He's not dead." The two hysterics exchange a series of "Fuck yous'. They start laughing. They keep laughing and Eddie sticks his head into the front seat. The man driving looks directly at him. Their eyes are four inches apart and they are laughing insanely. Inside of Eddie's head he is telling the man that he is the boss now. Without a word the maniacal face is answering,"Yes, I know you are, Eddie, for now." Eddie's red speed eyes are driving a hole into the driver's brain, his face a fun-house-mirror-contortion telling him, "You will do what I tell you." The man's laughter is subsiding. He's trying to calm down. He checks the road. In the windshield reflection Eddie sees the Federale's blood on half his face. He looks down at his hands and sees they are red. He wipes them in his hair. He says nothing more and pulls his head back into the camper like a dog coming out of a hole. He croaks, "It was him or us." It is so absurd they start laughing all over again. Eddie announces the plan they have already agreed upon, to make it his plan now. "Let's stash and switch and get back over the border." The driver nods his head, and casually locates the 45 under his seat with one hand. "How fast were you going?" The man shrugs disgustedly. His voice from the front seat echoes like the sound from a storm drain, sounds reminding Eddie of an emergency room gurney, or a voice from a nightmare. "What difference does it make?" Eddie feels something evil becoming aroused, as though a capacity for power he does not want is taking over, as though something wrong in him is the boss. He knows he has finally, completely, turned his back on himself when he says, "None, none at all."

Another six miles up the road they switch cars. Eddie sees the man going out the camper door again. He lights another joint. He's getting so tired – exhausted, and much too loaded to get anything resembling sleep. But he knows that he is asleep right now. Eddie stumbles out of the truck and holds out his hand to the man. "I'll drive." "No, you won't." "Yes, I will." The man hands over the keys. Eddie slides behind the wheel of the Porsche.

It's Le Mans over the Tecate hills. They gain speed as they approach the burning bails on either side of the road. The little shack has two Federale cars parked in front. They pass through at over a hundred miles an hour, a 45 weighing heavily in the wind out of each window. They fire off weird explosions that the car outruns immediately. Come and get us. Come and get us. Come and get us. By dawn they are in a third car holding nothing but cancelled bullfight tickets and what look like severe gringo hangovers. They pass the border with the guard giving them a casual wave. Back to Mars.

Unable to sleep, Eddie wants to see her. They go walking along the lawns surrounding Mission Bay. Her eyes are cool blue, icy. The smile is normal, the eyes are cold. Eddie sees it coming. He tries to get her to talk about it. She won't. Suddenly it's out. She's leaving for France. Eddie can't believe it, but something makes him cry. As he cries for this girl that means so little to him, he wonders how wigged out he must be. He doesn't love her. He doesn't love anything. Is that it? She purrs, "Poor baby," in a practiced tone that would seem sincere to a square, and should be an insult to Eddie. He doesn't even care. He keeps snivelling. "Fuck, what am I turning into?" She asks for his speed when they climb the beach house stairs into her studio, assuring him that she'll give it to him as soon as he wakes up. Yes, she knows how he gets. She'll be there, because she has to pack anyway. They go to bed. After the first time she asks him to take a shower. Eddie doesn't blame her. Before he finishes the next, he feels himself falling asleep, her beautiful vague body sliding away. She's sitting in a chair when he wakes up on Tuesday around dusk. Her feet whisper across the floor. Warm fresh squeezed orange juice, a handful of bennies, and she tells him she'll miss him. He'd better go though, her father is coming to take her to the airport. Going down the stairs he's glad that it's over. A man gets out of a Lincoln

Continental and passes Eddie at the foot of the stairs. He looks at Eddie, he looks at him again. Eddie says, "Yes, I am." The man says, "I thought so." Eddie walks back to his apartment behind the low-life beer hall that he thought was dangerous and interesting when he moved there two years ago, and now just smells like piss in the sun.

The next morning Eddie knows the man is dead as soon as he steps out of his door. Lying there motionless with the beach damp in little dots in his hair. Who needs to see his face? Bottle Chicano fought Red-freak last night and won. Bottle Chicano banged Red-freak's head too many times. Red-freak managed to get his headache and temper tantrum just this far, to the front door of Eddie's house in Old Mission. Eddie steps over him. It is now beyond his code to care about things like violent death. Fuck him, Eddie's roommate can call the cops. Eddie walks down the beach noticing the perfect sets rolling in, but he's a little hungover, and the speed makes him cold as hell in the water.

That night Eddie's with a new girl and yes, he is fronting a little. His Levis drag down too large. He wears a red waiter's jacket and no shirt. Eddie looks like a baboon with a huge head of tangled hair. A month ago he was at the Olympic trials, faking an injury when he couldn't get any higher on the speed he had left, and had nothing in reserve. Besides, he had himself convinced that the whole deal was a joke, supported by the kind of people that believed in the war, and his life contained the true life of the outlaw which meant he was really the winner. The predominant voice in his head kept telling him he was an asshole and would soon be dead, and fuck you, anyway. The new girl is rich, from Marin. She is tall, skinny, with the narrow rib cage and medium breasts that Eddie likes. Her mouth is huge and she smiles rarely, the lips are enough. Her infrequent smile is like punctuation, timed perfectly with an ironic observation. It was hard to say who hated themselves more, the girl with the money, or the boy suspended over the ground awaiting the next fall. They were young, they took what they had in common and tried to call it

119

love, or attraction, or some fucking thing. It didn't matter, they drank themselves to sleep and hated each other after they fucked, because it used to mean something with someone else and meant nothing now. But she'd let Eddie do anything, and she wanted him to. Eddie imitated her upperclass attitudes and style. She convinced him he was a coward, or he'd be dead already. But they walked like the proudest people on earth. The public must never know. And the public was aware of them. Wherever they went they carried a certain on-time charisma. The midnight rambler and a beautiful stray cat.

A Hell's Angel grabs his cock and groans at her as they walk past. Eddie is nuts to do this, so it is perfect. He walks back to him and says, "C'mere." The Angel stands stock still. Eddie slaps his face, calls him "...A fuckin' punk." Eddie has been eating steriods and speed for several weeks, strong and crazy. The Angel is no match. The Angels face is pouring blood in seconds. Eddie scares himself as he goes absolutely wild, transformed into an angry body, but sitting back with ice-cold emotions. It's as though Eddie is just above their heads watching two animals fighting in the street, but at the same time he feels his fists cracking the face of the Angel, turning it to mush. Eddie picks him up and runs with him. Wondering, what am I going to do next? He spins and throws the helpless Angel in front of a carload of tourists, as the near unconcious body bounces off the fender and lies there, Eddie screams he's not hurt and starts kicking him. He wonders, in the semi-quiet part of his brain, if he is going to kill him, surprised that he wants to kill him. The girl is holding and doesn't want the cops, she grabs Eddie's arm and pulls him off. Eddie wants to leave before any other Angels see this. They drive up to Del Mar and pick at their food on a deck over looking the setting sun, drinking Tequila and feeling aroused.

For the next six weeks, Eddie is pursued by Angels. He sleeps in a new place every night, his cars are broken into, his bed is set on fire, his new girl gets raped and leaves town.

Eddie moves to Logan Heights in the riot-burned section

of the ghetto. He is not wanted there, he looks like trouble. Nevertheless there are a series of parties, the house is a clearing room for speed and marijuana. Eddie beats his roommate's dog. He stays in the house for two days with the cowering dog lying in the kitchen. Eddie scalds his hands in the sink. He cries and wonders what he has become. He stops crying. He sits. He cries some more. He knows he is just too pissed. He goes down the list, naming everything but himself.

He's got another run to make tomorrow. Back at the hovel at the beach he stays up drinking, smoking dope, lifting weights and listening to "Gimme Shelter" over and over again. He's half hoping this will be the time and he can take a few with him. Scared into a stinking cold sweat, the volume of everything is much too loud.

To his surprise, when he's sitting on the cliff five miles north of the campground where he first saw Jenny ten years earlier, he misses his mother. He misses her the whole time he waits; he misses her like a little boy. He sits on the cliff waiting for the speedboat, mindlessly packaging the bricks, setting the net, watching for the flashlight signals, hoping the Federales haven't learned the spot and signal... to lure him out there, to shoot him in the water and let him bloat, and be found by some surf fisherman like the guy before him. The white light blinks about a hundred yards off shore. Eddie will never let go of the load, he knows the only respect anyone has left for him comes from those that can respect craziness. If he drowns they'll find the net with him. He takes the gaffer tape and weaves his fingers into the net, a handhold he can't let go. He jumps. Eddie, and a net of two hundred bricks wrapped in plastic, drops down the black cliff and splashes next to the rocks below. Coming to the surface and slamming into the rocks under the force of angry white water, Eddie looks at the boat, recognizes it and swims toward it, dragging his load, laughing.

He hasn't been in his old house since his father told him he'd turn him into the FBI if he could tell them where to find him.

His mother looks at him like he's a ghost. She stands there by the door, nodding her head: Yes. Yes. This is what you've become. She knew it all the time. Yes. Yes. This is you. THIS is NOT me. I am temporarily living this. I am partial; this is NOT the whole story. It is what I have to DO, not what I have BECOME. Can't you see that? No, she can't. She nods her head — cold as ice, unfeeling. Yes. Yes. Look at yourself. Eddie tells her, "I missed you." She says, "That's good, now leave." As he leaves, he hears her crying, heading for her bedroom.

He winds up delivering some dope to a fraternity house that is holding some afternoon party. The frat boys think Eddie is some kind of romantic figure, they get some vicarious rush out of being close to him. They promote him to some of the girls in an effort to keep him around. Besides, Eddie gets good drugs. There are some great looking girls there, some of them curious about Eddie, most of them pushovers for anything he'd tell them. They're too young to see through the outlaw front, never guessing he'd just been put down by his mother. Eddie talks to a few of them looking for some sign of decadence in their faces, some giveaway that his being with them would not be the low mark of their lives. No luck. His soul is in a drought and the mark is even lower than he thought.

Just before he leaves, a guy walks up. Eddie knows the guy is a narc and tells him so. Eddie feels something gaining strength, feels an expansion of some wrong-headed need, blames it on the narc, tells him if he sees him again, he'll kill him. Eddie swallows a lump, knowing that he really means it and that he really will. Eddie knows that he has finally given up. It is a weird perverse freedom finally getting to that place. To have that power, not over the narc, over himself. Eddie knows he'll throw it all away now, at the drop of a hat. He'll stand in the moat and yell "Fuck the King." Eddie spends a little more time convincing the narc, who needs no convincing. The narc can see it in Eddie's eyes, smells it coming through his skin. The narc is never seen around again.

Eddie likes the fear he brings where ever he goes. Because

Eddie has realized he is entirely powerless. Empty. Dead already. Just breathing. The war rages on, the killing reverberates just over the heads of the whole world, no one escapes it. The war makes a lie of anyone still breathing, no one deserves to breathe, no one can stop the killing, and until the killing stops everyone and everything is rotting like a corpse in the sun. Eddie feels it as a total humiliation; if this is what it's about, then someone oughta kill him now and get it over with. Let 'em try. It's all cheap, blood spent for nothing.

The last run was closer than any – won't be long now. He's rolling joints for a few friends. Smiling in secret amazement at the physics of simply not caring, and how that seems to break the odds wide open. Despite everything, Eddie is still breathing. The room is full of young long-haired friends, some of them radical-left professors, a pimp and two prostitutes, kids from the neighborhood, a buddy and three new girls and another narc. Eddie has been sloppy. He doesn't realize the long haired rat-faced guy is a narc until six cops carrying shotguns walk through the screen door, and the sound of a helicopter begins whopping over the house. The cops ask whose Galaxy is parked down the street. Eddie says, "Mine." Well, it is being used to hold up gas stations. "It is?" Yes. "When?" At night, around 2 or 3 in the morning. "Yeah?" Yeah. "That's when I come home from the job I have, parking cars in Mission Valley." Silence. "That's a bad time to be driving." That's right. "It's a bad car to be driving." Silence. "I won't be driving that car anymore. In fact, I'll be leaving town. Tonight, this afternoon." "That's a good idea." They leave, the narc leaves with them. One cop lingers behind. He's a skinny guy looking and sounding like Hank Williams. He looks so pissed, like he's going to start crying. He tells Eddie, "If I ever catch you again with drugs..." He stops and his Adam's apple jumps up and down his throat as he regains his composure. His voice gains control and Eddie recognizes his face from someplace. He finishes emphatically, "...If I ever see you again, I'm going to send you straight to the place where scum like you belong." Eddie smiles at him. The cop catches his breath and tries to get outside. He can't, and slams the door shut. Eddie's heart flies through the roof. He fights off the desire to placate the enraged Okie. The cop's face is shaking under the skin. His eyes are looking at Eddie with a kind of panic. Eddie wonders if the cop knows that the barrel of the shot-gun is traveling toward Eddie's chest. Eddie knows that another instant of insolence will drive the cop over the edge, he thinks "Fuck it, – him or me." Eddie sucks his teeth and smiles again. The cop seems to lift off the floor, but he begins to back out the door. Eddie sees him killing him in a raid, or for any excuse. Eddie locks his eyes on the cop, who is staring back promising Eddie silently that he will do what he says he will do. Eddie says, "I don't care, I don't give a fuck."

Eddie drives up to Marin, north of San Francisco that night, listening to "Stairway To Heaven" between static on the radio. Oddly, he turns off the exit and makes it to 29th and California to visit a woman he'd met who he has been thinking about a lot. He wants to see her again and get her off his mind. Just see her, sleep with her, talk to her and see that she's another girl, someone else he can leave, and won't need. He makes it to her house, she lets him in, he never leaves.

WHAT'D YA SAY?

The next time Eddie said "I don't give a fuck", and thought he meant it was to his wife. Despite, and because of, his love of his wife and his daughter – he resented them and regarded himself as a coward for the attachments he had toward them. His external world was no longer a battlefield. His simple freedom to risk life or death was changed to stupid domestic quarrels and self-hatred. Unable to express himself as a husband or father he plunged into a darker and darker depression.

The shades of the bedroom were drawn against the warm sun beating on the window. His wife walked into the room holding a picture of Eddie when he was a fifth grader. "Look at him. Look at that eager face. What has become of you? What do you want to do with your life?" It wasn't a cop cradling a shotgun this time, it was his beautiful wife of 12 years. Eddie felt the same emotion as he had when the shotgun slowly turned toward his chest, foolishly he told the same lie, the one he still thought he believed, "I don't give a fuck." In three weeks she was gone, and he blamed her.

What'd ya say? Sorry. Why do I live in the desert? You want to know that, huh. Why I live in the desert? I started living out here, a little while after, a long time ago, when...

I'd been driving all night, in a very dark, very solitary car. You can feel alone that way. I was driving, I was real tired, strained. I started seeing things. It was the last few minutes of night, right before dawn.

I saw a floor-to-ceiling off-white curtain blowing rhythmi-cally in the sunlight. The windows were open and the breeze felt as though I were actually in the room. But I wasn't, I was still in the car. Then I heard a bird calling from a distance, a long distance.

I could see the bird stop, stare around, then flip its head up and call out a combination of a song and a cry. The bird was perched on a tall century plant. Each time it sang, it bounced gently on the branch.

I heard murmuring. Then a single loud laugh from the cool shady side of the room. A woman's laugh. I heard kisses softly exchanged. First one, then another. I heard more murmuring, a kiss and a sound in my wife's throat, a deeply satisfied rumble. Mary was walking to the window. The curtains licked her legs, swung around her and clung to her briefly. The curtain seemed transparent, Mary an apparition.

She is beautiful. Radiant. She is happy, Delirious. She is the same and entirely different. Transformed. She stands in an unfamiliar posture of security and strength, drawn from her lover, given to her lover, given to herself. She is free. Feeling at last a time where she belongs, a place she loves, a self to love. The exhilaration of being where she is, where it had seemed for so long impossible to be.

Mary stares out the window. Her brown eyes languish, deeply relaxed, alert, encompassing everything. The still of the morning, the permanence of the desert. She believes what is in front of her, what she can see. She teases herself thinking that the woman on the bed behind her is not really there. Her heart pounds for a second. She turns and her eyes meet the eyes of another woman. The woman smiles, and smiles again. The impulse of a warm electric twitch throbs between their legs. The look in each other's eyes. Mary remembers taking her lover in her arms, her legs in her legs, her mouth in her mouth. In a post orgasm choreography, they inhale, they exhale, they smile. Beautiful mirror images.

A knock on the door. The maid. "Come in." Comfortable together in their nakedness, they laugh at the absurdity of covering themselves in this room, their room.

I walk in. The room becomes a swirling centrifuge of emotion. I start to shake, I lose my voice. I suddenly become tired, defeated, desperate.

I look at Mary. I tell her, "I'm sorry. I had to see you. I had to see the reality. The images were so strong that I thought the reality would be better." The reality is not better. I feel foolish. The women come to my aid. They prop me up with their compassionate faces. They register my pain. They want me to be strong. My desperation is a foreign echo to them and it is amplified by a series of dull explosions in my chest.

"I'm sorry, I gotta go," I say. Mary stands silent by the curtain, almost invisible in the light. She is illuminated in the curtain. She is veiled by the bright sunlight. I cannot move to her. I will break down in a useless series of pleads and sobs.

From the bed, from my wife's lover's lips to my ears, a sound from deep in her chest, "Do you want to talk?" she asks like she means it. I can see she regrets the question. Without saying a word she is telling me, "No. Go. Leave now. You don't belong here."

"No, I can't talk. I had to come here. It's like an amputation. Nobody really believes it even after it happens. It makes you sick and fevered not to believe something like that, not until they pull the sheets down, and you see what you have to see to believe it."

Five miles up the road, I see in the room again. I see Mary crying. The woman gets up from the bed and embraces her saying nothing. The curtains sway, Mary sobs. The woman holds her close. The woman kisses her eyes, her ears, her mouth. They fall into each other.

I can't leave the room. I try to put my thoughts in Mary's head. I want her to think of the twelve years with me. They are gasping. I want their love to have some connection to me. Even if it means she is tearing my fetters to pieces, pulsating through my remembered irritability, my condescending understanding, my denials. I want her to exorcise my demands, my bullying. I want her to smother my injustices, to shudder past my protests. I see her body pressing, pushing, spreading, and convulsing like an elevator screaming past the familiar floors, beyond the roof, into the air.

In a medium faint, she falls asleep, sweat running rivulets down her swollen neck, across her open arm pits, spotting the sheets. She moans. She has a dream of when she was a little girl with a very high temperature. Then I go into her dream. I dream of her dreaming of me. From another time. My familiar profile with the scenery changing behind me. She sees me force a smile. In a tone as though she were offering me coffee on a long drive, sitting beside me in the car, invisible a few inches away, I hear Mary's voice say, "Time heals all wounds."

I hear the woman's voice breathe in my love's ear, "That's right."

ROBERT, I KNOW
WHEN I'M NOT WANTED...

I was pretty scared even before the lights went out. The party had turned from "soul shakes," and "Como está, amigo?" to "Why don't we send these white boys to the hospital?" We were where we didn't belong, and it was too late to do anything about it. It was our own fault; we'd pulled out some drugs, assuming they would be welcome. They weren't welcome and neither were we.

We'd been trying to make as casual an exit as possible for the last minute or two, but the rapidly accumulating insults and jeers were making it clear that there was a penalty charged against us, and our sentences were going to be worked out informally. But severely.

Chris had his hands stuffed in his pockets as he rocked back and forth on his heels, trying to seem calm, while the expression on his face was telling Robert and me, "I told you guys to just buy a record; you didn't have to mainline your ethnic fix."

Robert got jostled from behind and fell into a large and humorless man with a recently shaved head. His scalp, criss-crossed with old scars, was flaky with scabs and had a tattoo crucifix over one side. He had tattooed tears running from one eye and had lost an ear someplace. The man turned and thumped Robert hard on the chest. Robert backed up, slowly shaking his lowered head as he tossed his hands in the air, saying, "Qué pasa?"

"Qué pasa?" mimicked a girl who had been quite friend-ly to us in the minutes before we pulled out the blow. In that instant, the entire room had frozen. Here we'd been, the three of us, sitting on the couch with the stupid smiles melting on our faces. Our eightball in it's zipped baggie slumped on the coffee table. Twenty cold and disgusted faces staring at the bag, then at each other and then at us with a collective menace that was, as I said before, pretty scary.

I put my hand inside my jacket as though I were carrying a gun, thinking at the time, "This is stupid, they'll think you're going for your badge." They knew we weren't armed; I don't know how. I felt like a fraternity boy whose car had broken down in a "bad" section of town. We rose to our feet in unison. No one else in the room budged, except to raise their heads as their eyes followed us to our full height. Robert reached down, snapped the baggie off the table and put it into his jacket pocket. I almost said, "Welp, I guess we'll be going then..," but before I could get it out of my mouth, the guy with the tattooed tears was introducing himself to Robert.

Everyone was on their feet; the weight of the crowd was pressing in on us. The room began to stink with the smell of fight or flight. I glanced at Chris, who managed another tight-lipped smile as he rolled his eyes heavenward, finally focusing on Robert, who was by now on the other side of the room. Robert's dance partner was trying to break his ribs with frequent and devastating explosions..

No one spoke loudly. There were just the sounds of sarcastic muttering and a ridgid mocking attitude combining with the thuds on Robert's chest every five or six seconds. In silence our captors began shifting positions, cutting off any chance for escape and separating us from each other. One guy I knew didn't like me even before the room turned ugly, and a particularly beautiful and belligerent girl, worked their way behind me.

I had picked her out the second I walked in the door. We exchanged smiles before I realized that the pair of eyes I felt pinning me from her left belonged to her boyfriend. Under normal circumstances things would have been cool as long as I never looked at the girl again, and avoided any chance encounters in hallways or bedrooms, or at the refrigerator. She was fairly small, in tight black jeans, wearing cowboy boots. She had on a light-blue cowboy shirt with snap buttons. Her breasts were putting those buttons to the test and the first four from the top had already given up. She had large white teeth and a lovely mouth which smiled in a way that stunned me. It was an entirely sexual smile, a knowing smile. Now her eyes were not smiling; her eyes were cold analysts that missed nothing, and found very little in me to appreciate. She and her boyfriend were on the same wavelength. I had clearly fucked up. The girl poked me in the ribs under my armpit a few times, hissing, "Hey, fock you, man. Hey, fock you, asshole. Hey, fock you, man," in an odd sort of rhythmic chant. The guy was a classic "vato loco": compact, durable, tough, with no nervous system to speak of. He didn't say anything; he was pressing his weight against me so I'd lose my balance and he could use my sudden movement as an excuse to attack. I figured I had much less than a minute. I couldn't think of a thing to do or a thing to say.

Then the lights went out. Somebody grabbed the collar of my jacket. I tucked my chin down firm on my neck to take the blade across my chin and jaw instead of my throat. My mouth suddenly got warm and I swallowed a mouthful of blood. I grabbed the girl and bearhugged her in front of me. She was reaching back over her head, pulling my hair and filling her fingernails with skin she tore off my face. The guy who was cutting me couldn't find the place he was looking for. The girl started howling in Spanish. Her body jumped and twisted in my arms as she absorbed the impact of the knife targeted for my stomach and chest.

I heard Chris shouting instructions to Robert, urging him to get over to the window in the corner of the room. I heard the sound of the window pane breaking. I was too far away. If I followed I'd be certain to be caught up in the pursuit of my friend. I started to back up, offering no resistance to the bodies shoving past me toward the sound of the breaking glass.

The boyfriend was muttering something to the girl in my arms, but she wasn't responding coherently. While he tried to figure out what was wrong, I kept backing up. The far side of the black room grew quiet. It contained a confusing sound of grunts, thuds and expelled breath. I was sure they had Chris and Robert on the floor. I kept backing up.

Finally all the bodies behind me were gone and I lost my balance with the sudden release of pressure from the moving wall of people. I stumbled backward into the kitchen. The voice of the guy with the knife revealed that he knew something was real wrong, but that voice was going to sound a lot worse when he found out for sure. I held the girl as tightly as I could to prevent her from inhaling enough air to find words. Somehow she managed to get my hand between her teeth as I twisted her head back and sideways. She got loose for a second and inhaled before I rammed the palm of my hand under her chin and twisted her head again. I felt and heard a deep pop in her shoulder, and her body dropped heavily into shock. I let go of her with one hand, propped her up for a second and hit her as hard as I could in the face, pushing her against the doorjam we had just fallen through.

The kitchen was empty except for the sound of two men breathing hard. I could hear them coming closer and tried to place the sound of their shuffling feet. I was frantically feeling the walls for a door or a window. I thought the thin cool handle might be to the refrigerator, but in my panic I yanked on it before I could stop myself.

The refrigerator light threw a dim rectangle, revealing for a second the red girl in the fetal position in the doorway and two guys blinking at me.

I glimpsed another door in the corner and jumped for it. I pushed with all my strength, but it opened to the inside. Then I pulled on it before I turned the knob. The men started screaming for their friends. As the door finally opened, one of the guys climbed on my back, wrapping his arms around my head. The other guy slid along the floor, hanging on to one of my legs; I kicked backward and dented his forehead with the sharp edge of my boot. I turned sideways and tried to scrape the other man, who should have been a jockey, off on the door jam. I tried to finish the man on the floor with one final kick, but my foot swung wide and glanced the side of his face. I lost my balance and rose into the air, and then began falling onto my back, with the guy still clamped around my shoulders. I landed hard and felt the air leave his body, as my weight deflated his chest. I could see his eyes bug out and hear his desperate gasps for air as we lay on the floor. He was tough as hell and his fingers still felt like steel talons on my neck; I began twisting his thumb and fingers in all the directions they weren't suppposed to go, and broke free.

I rolled out the kitchen door, got to my feet and fell down the concrete porch onto the sidewalk. I jumped up, slipped on the wet lawn and made it away from the house by crawling, running on all fours and staggering to a fence. I half-jumped, half-climbed over the chain links, dropping flat on my back into someone's yard. A couple of large pit bulls came streaking at me, barking and growling.

JUMPER

He rolled the car window down with one hand, drove the car with the other. The sound of the hissing tires on the wet asphalt invigorated him. Being invigorated was not beneficial. Invigorated only meant amplified, and this was the last thing he wanted or needed.

He'd been in an emotional state for months, perhaps years, a state in which slivers of occurrences or actions that remained incomplete would erupt very disconnected feelings in him. The confusion and exhaustion made him feel utterly useless and lost.

These sensations were common; they were the central part of his life, except for a dull, muted sense of panic during increasing anxiety or fatigue. The panic was muted because he had grown accustomed to its clockwork regularity – at intervals three times per night as he slept, and again at dawn. It occurred repeatedly each time throughout the day when he saw a familiar face. It occurred each time his daughter or his wife initiated a conversation with him.

The fear always precipitated a strange series of impressions, some of which were so odd that for a moment they would hold his interest. He would want to construct something out of these images, visions, theories – but being without a sense of who he was, he could not.

He'd made the mistake of trying to communicate these impressions, but for the past few days he had given up. He chose instead to be silent, or he would try to read, in an attempt to arrange the feelings and thoughts into some logical sequence by simply following the writer's sentences across the page. He hoped this would make his struggle less apparent to others.

His wife and daughter began to comment that he seemed remote – "not there." He could not explain. He simply shrugged, hoping that it might pass as a denial.

In past attempts to communicate, he had often felt physically ill. As he watched his wife or daughter trying to make sense of his statements, he would be overwhelmed with sadness. He would nod his head in agreement with the rational sense of their views. It was impossible for him to point to the emotional confusion and desperation with which each of their observations struck him. He felt like a short kid riding a huge pretend horse in blinding circles, grabbing for an impossible ring.

He was ashamed as he observed them losing their time and energy in efforts to translate his words and impressions into something that had meaning. He watched them working at finding bogus meanings that offered hope or made simple sense, offered an object lesson or gave some insight. Minutes became hours as he watched one or the other trying to point to a path that might offer relief. He knew there was no relief.

The sound of the hissing tires, the predawn fog, the bridge he was driving over and the cyclone fence above the sidewalk on the outside edge of the rail brought a hallucination.

In front of his eyes he could see the rings of a tree like those at the end of a sawed log. He knew immediately what the image meant. It referred to ego, the core of something real, an ego with surrounding enclosed rings. Each ring represented the time that has surrounded that ego and each ring further from the core was another period of survival. It seemed so pointless.

He pulled his car over and set the emergency brake. He felt mean. He became furious. He thought he would turn out the lights in an attempt to cause a pile-up on the narrow lane. He wanted to add the message of anger to his passing. Feeling that his daughter would have a hard enough time coping with his coming action, he decided that it would prove he loved her if he turned the blinking lights on.

He realized he would have to move fast. He pounced on the

cyclone fence, feeling the weight of his body pulling his fingers in the wire diamonds. His feet slipped. He remembered the many times he had hit a fence on a dead run, agile and quick, climbing to the top and dropping off to the other side, into another place where he did not belong. He slipped again. His heart sank. Bungling and awkward, he felt humiliated. He kept climbing, determined to do this, once and for all. He began to blame his slipping and his clumsy effort on the wetness of the fence, his years out of practice, but he was not convinced. Dispirited, he slid down the face of the fence, catching his wedding ring behind the wire, and tearing skin loose from one knuckle. As he sprawled on the concrete at the foot of the fence, he laughed until he cried.

He watched a couple of cars changing lanes as they approached his parked car. He walked in front of his own headlights as they blazed impersonally against his thighs. He swung open the car door, got into the car, and with his heart pounding hard, drove across the bridge.

A helicopter was streaking toward the bridge from the Coast Guard Station a mile away. As the crew saw the car pulling off they radioed up to a Highway Patrol car, "Looks like the jumper has changed his mind. Why don't you guys pull him over and see how he's doing?" The car radioed back, "Will do, thanks, Fellas." "No problem."

NEAR THE EQUINOX

The floor of the room must have been made of dry ice. I wondered how powerful the light had to be in order to illuminate it from below. Something down there was burning hot. This dark room filled with ankle high mist, suggesting hell, seemed like a place I had been before and, worse, like a place I belonged. The cold mists rising in thundering red flashes looked like the stage effect from a production at the Old Globe Theatre near the bell tower in Balboa Park. With that thought, my lips began to form a smile, as another black-out seized me.

I shielded my eyes against the silver glare of an old house trailer. As I moved out of the direct glare, a boy backed down the metal stairs. He was unwinding a steel measuring tape attached to the kitchen faucet inside. He backed up slowly, counting his steps as he went. He ran into the trailer and came out with an old camera. He took close-up shots of every footprint he'd made beside the tape. The camera clicked in the dark nine times. A voice said, "What goes on up there, is determined by what happens down here." Sawdust blew over the footprints, and I blacked out again.

A voice with the confidence and the certainty of adolescence demanded my attention. I couldn't concentrate. A blinding headache moaned slowly and stretched a brutal hand downward into nausea. A face in a pilot's helmet searched the dark water below, his voice was drowned in the sound of the blades beating in the dark. A kid's voice rose above the noise as the copter banked off to the left shutting off its searchlight. I attempted some kind of denial. The voice wouldn't let me finish. He was saying, "No, you won't. I'll never let you. How high do you think you'll get off your knees like that ?"

Dry ice again. The girls and boys were dancing in a slow shuffle, stirring those mists into silent, scorching cyclones which rose to the level of their hips. I heard my own voice: "Where am I?" Warm womens' voices mixed laughing, "Oklahoma," "It must be yours," and "Time heals all wounds." I blacked out again.

She always wore those black pumps. Her hips were enveloped in a tight dress. With me in tan corduroy Levis and a pair of old shoes, the kind with the basset hound in the heel, we wound clockwise in a tight, hot circle. A saxophone rumbled a melody that sounded like the initial moments of sex. Her foot planted between my feet, our weight rocking left and right, back and forth. My heart ached deeper and harder, breathing became impossible. The pain climbed until I feared a nocturnal heart attack. It was soul, not body. Before the images faded, something brushed my lips lightly; I smelled her sweat and skin. Her lipstick tasted vague. My erection began its silent pounding. She whispered, "You didn't keep your promise." I blacked out.

A cat started yeowling in an empty metal storage house. This set off the dogs barking furiously. As the sound grew beyond what the cavernous room could contain, I tried to shut off the hose, thinking it was the source of my nightmare. Outside in the wind-whipped, tall rustling grass, a huge cat coughed a warning. The dogs and everything else alive accelerated into a hysterical retreat. Razor talons pulled down a huge ghost. The grass spun crazily in the wind. The legs of the ghost kicked frantically in the dust before me. The narrator had a boy's voice: "This is not me. This is what I have become." One cat eye stared at me until everything was cold and black again.

My face was hot, my lips salty. The kid who had been speaking was finally revealed leaning against a camper, picking at a bit of athletic tape he had wrapped around one finger. He slouched on his hip, implying an androgeny. He stared up angrily at that thought, then relaxed into an amused sneer. He spat through his teeth and warned "Don't get me wrong." I knew the look, having used it every minute of my life. He was insolent, standing in the hot sunlight treating a severe sunburn as a matter of course, as though the hot red skin and swollen eyelids had nothing to do with anything.

I was impressed with his self-possession. He'd been dealt a strong hand, or at least had the confident manner that implied he had access to one. He had an attitude of expectation that followed an adherence to some type of code. I couldn't remember it. He stared at me for what seemed like years. During those decades it became apparent that he was locked in a struggle, completely misplaced in the bowels of my own prison. He told me I had introduced his torturers as my guests. I tried to apologize. He laughed and said "Save it. You'll need it later." He stood there mocking what I had become, while he inhaled honor and exhaled humility. He told me I hadn't listened to anyone but the voices planted in my own head by my own disrespect: "Ya turned on me." At the precise instant I tried to use him as something to envy, continuing to poison what remained of my soul, he interrupted me with a wave of his hand. He turned his head suddenly as though he had heard a summons. I blacked out.

I wanted a drink. I wanted to wear old boots and find a sawdust floor and exchange a glance with a hungry woman. I wanted to find the unspoken promise and set the trap. I wanted to fall. I wanted to burn. It almost doubled me over. If I couldn't play it, I wanted to hear it. If I couldn't have it, I wanted to see it. If I couldn't do it, I wanted to fake it. It felt like the last twenty years of my life had vanished. The kid's voice: "Weak. You forgot the seasons, you forgot to breathe in the available air." I began to whine in embarrassment. The kid asked me with an incredulous tone, "What happened to you?" I blacked out.

"He's gonna come back." I didn't know if it was a promise or a warning. I began to feel the pain of circulation coming back to frozen limbs. A dreadful and welcome pain. Almost too much to stand. As she continued speaking I opened my eyes to her retreating face. She stood far out in the middle of a dance floor. I walked to her and wrapped my arms around her; the fit seemed perfect. Shadows danced around us, most of them limping and trying to support each other. I could smell blood and disease. I heard muffled sobbing. The mists covered us again. I'd forgotten how beautiful she was. Her face changed gradually from one girl to another, from the girls I had known to the women I wanted to know. The process seemed to take hours. Her body constantly crossed the line and became mine, and pulled away and became her own. I was on the edge of orgasm.

I felt like an imposter, a stand-in, as though I would be discovered any second in a humiliating mistake. She held me tighter and convulsed in my arms. I was afraid to believe that she was still here with me after all this time. I wanted to say something, but I knew it would be stupid. I couldn't find any words. She did. She said, "You're one and the same." She smiled briefly, then leaned further into my ear. Her breath was hot and her sweating face made her words moist as she whispered, "You're making too big a deal outta this." She vanished.

I ran in circles until the dogs were too tired to keep up and howled at me from a distance, enraged that I had escaped. I crept into a grass field as the sun dropped like a stone down a well. I stumbled in the waist-high swirling grass and began to part the field with my hands as the dogs behind me gained ground. Dead white faces at my feet, with blue foaming lips, tried to say my name. I blacked out again. For an hour I heard my father's dog tags jangling as he ran ahead of me.

Pitch black. Dim red light. Close quarters, sulfur, muffled prayers. Felt like a couple of hundred degrees. The trick was to keep breathing, in and out, in and out – the slightest pause and I was sure to ignite. I smelled burning hair, it was that close. The kid dragged the chair across my mother's kitchen floor. He sat on the kitchen table and as my eyes adjusted to the dark, his murky form emerged, perched like a statue supporting his head in his hands. I thought of infrared sights and snipers.

He looked up at me. I remembered being eighteen and rushing with the onset of hallucination, how I'd go find a mirror and stare into it, saying, "So that's what you look like." It was him. He grew impatient. " You ignored everything you knew to be true. I wish you'd had more balls. You lost your nerve, forgot all the rhythm and timing, the seasons, stopped counting on your own sense of what to do next. Why did you listen to all of that bullshit, all those times you doubted yourself." He lost control and hammered me in the sternum with his fist. It felt like I was being slaughtered. We coughed blood over the table and bent over in agony.

He paused for a second. We regained our composure. I thought for a minute he wasn't going to finish what he was trying to say. He held that pause the way one who loves you pauses before she tells you she has caught you in a lie. The moments crawled in that strained manner that takes hold when you receive the news of a loved one's death." We were always afraid, and always will be. But fear alone doesn't make you a coward." He began to calm down. A streetlight went off outside the window. It began to rain. Single early-morning lights went on in the windows of dark houses perched on in the surrounding canyons. I walked over to the screen door smelling the rain on the asphalt mixing with the deep green moisture lifting from the lawn, nearly tasting the seductive air from the jasmine tree. A warm wind blew down from the hillside. I heard jeering voices calling me in the distance. Although he didn't raise his voice, but of course he didn't have to, his words drowned out the dark jeers. "They try to make us all declare some kind of war on someone, or something. Your war was on me."

It was as though his hatred vanished when he seemed certain I understood his meaning. We began to gain power. I felt speed and strength returning to my body. I heard the sound of my own voice above the din of the terrified enraged voices screaming conflicting instructions. My fingers became talons clutching my bleeding soul. I was again airborne when he said, "It's the middle of summer, your season. Mine was spring."

SPECIAL THANKS ~

Carol Fregly
(and her students at San Francisco City College)

Joe Hancock + 1

Mason Jones

Jo Mancuso

Dawn Holliday

Voorhees Mount

Alexis Paris

Sandra Verhoogen
(and her students at San Francisco City College, and Sky line College)

To anyone who has taken a friend into the
Hotel Terminus for a cup of coffee

And with respect and fond regards to anyone who
recognizes themself in these stories